"I'm sorry, Chase," she whispered.

"Shh," he breathed, and held her. Damn, she was breaking his heart. "We've both made mistakes, Mal. I have to take some blame, too. If I hadn't left you back then…if I'd stayed…" He wasn't about to tell her that he'd returned only to find she was already married, and all he could do was walk away from her a second time.

Mallory raised her head and looked at him, her green eyes luminous. "No. I knew all along how much you wanted to be a ranger. And you are such a good one." She touched his face, and he about lost it. "And you're a good man, too."

What he was feeling and thinking right now was far from being good. "And you're a good mother." He couldn't resist her any longer, and briefly touched his mouth to hers.

"Chase…"

"Quiet, Mal. We've talked enough." His mouth closed over hers, and he forgot about everything else but the woman in his arms.

Dear Reader,

This is a first for me. I've written numerous Western stories over the years, and several of the locations were in Texas, but I've never written a Texas Ranger as a hero.

I have to admit I was a little intimidated by their reputation alone. And I wasn't quite sure what exactly their job entailed. Was it more of an honorary position? Did these men, and now women, just walk around wearing white hats and a silver badge?

Then I talked with Carol Mathis, Administrative Technician for Ranger Company E in Midland, Texas. She eagerly answered all my questions about this elite group of 116 lawmen and women. The Rangers have protected the people of Texas since 1823. Their jobs include anything from going after kidnappers and bank robbers to helping find missing people. No job is too small or too large for a Texas Ranger. And, when it's needed, they still climb on a horse to go after the bad guy.

In my story, *Texas Ranger Takes a Bride,* Chase Landon goes in search of a boy who's been kidnapped by escaped convicts. The stakes are raised when he learns the child is his own son. Mallory Hagan, the woman he once loved but walked away from to become a Ranger, never told him of the boy. Now they have to put the past behind them and work together.

Once again it's been my privilege to learn about the Texas Rangers. They are truly heroes. Thanks, Carol, for all your help.

Any mistakes in this story are mine and mine alone.

Enjoy

Patricia Thayer

PATRICIA THAYER

Texas Ranger Takes a Bride

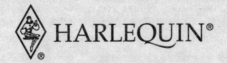

TORONTO • NEW YORK • LONDON
AMSTERDAM • PARIS • SYDNEY • HAMBURG
STOCKHOLM • ATHENS • TOKYO • MILAN • MADRID
PRAGUE • WARSAW • BUDAPEST • AUCKLAND

ISBN-13: 978-0-373-17538-3
ISBN-10:   0-373-17538-8

TEXAS RANGER TAKES A BRIDE

First North American Publication 2008.

This edition published by arrangement with Harlequin Books S.A.

® and TM are trademarks of the publisher. Trademarks indicated with ® are registered in the United States Patent and Trademark Office, the Canadian Trade Marks Office and in other countries.

www.eHarlequin.com

Printed in U.S.A.

Thanks to the understanding men in her life—
her husband of more than thirty-five years, Steve,
and her three grown sons and three grandsons—
Patricia Thayer has been able to fulfill her dream
of writing. Besides writing romance, she loves to
travel—especially in the West, where she researches
her books first hand. You might find her on a
ranch in Texas, or on a train to an old mining town
in Colorado, and this year you'll find her on an
adventure in Scotland. Just so long as she can share
it all with her favorite hero, Steve. She loves to hear
from readers. You can write to her at P.O. Box 6251,
Anaheim, CA 92816-0251, or check her Web site at
www.patriciathayer.com for upcoming books.

Patricia Thayer's popular series
THE TEXAS BROTHERHOOD
is back by popular demand!
Coming in January and March 2009—
catch up with the family and meet Luke and Brady.

January:
Luke: The Cowboy Heir

March:
Brady: The Rebel Rancher

To Helen,
I loved your fierce loyalty to your family
and friends, your joy for life, your bright smile
and your special way with words.
And I'll miss you, my friend.
Gentle Persuader, Helen Haddad,
June 13, 1933—October 17, 2007

CHAPTER ONE

SHE HADN'T BEEN ABLE to shake the uneasy feeling.

Mallory Hagan looked out the kitchen window toward the barn and corral area. Still no sign of Buck and Ryan. She trusted her father to take care of her eight-year-old son, but that didn't stop her from worrying.

On the plus side, he was a good rider, and his grandpa had taken him out on the trail many times. Just not overnight.

And never had they been four hours overdue.

Mallory paced the large ranch kitchen and stopped at the wall phone. Unable to stop herself, she picked up the receiver and called her dad's cell phone. It went right to voice mail…again. They must be in a dead area.

She looked up when the housekeeper, Rosalie, walked into the kitchen. "Still no sign of them?"

Mallory shook her head. "I'm getting concerned."

"Do you think Buck is checking his watch? No. He has his grandson out there, teaching him the cowboy way of life."

Over the years the housekeeper's once rich brown

hair had turned salt and pepper. It was pulled back into a no-nonsense ponytail, revealing warm hazel eyes and defined cheekbones. Rosalie Dudley had been the only other female in the house since the death of Mallory's mother over fifteen years ago. Mallory loved her like a second mother.

"So you're saying I'm being overprotective."

Rosalie smiled. "No, I'm just saying Buck wouldn't let anything happen to the boy. You two are his life."

Buck Kendrick owned a lot of land in this part of West Texas. On his forty-three sections he ran a large cattle operation, along with numerous oil wells, dotting the mostly barren landscape of mesquite, ocotillo cactus and buffalo grass that survived the area's lack of rainfall.

Mallory knew her father would give it all up to have his wife by his side, and another half-dozen kids to inherit what he'd worked so hard to build. But she was his only child, and Ryan his only grandchild. And since her husband's death, there weren't going to be any more children. Sadness welled inside Mallory as she recalled her turbulent marriage to Alan. Toward the end she'd feared for her and her son's safety.

Living outside of Lubbock, Texas, she'd been able to play the part of the dutiful wife. And keep Buck from knowing the truth about her husband's drinking and incomprehensible actions.

She brushed aside the thought. "You know, Dad isn't as young as he used to be."

"You better not let Buck hear you say that."

Mallory smiled. "Well, he still does too much. And I'm afraid he's going to show off for Ryan."

"Probably, but he's got Joe and Mick with him," Rosalie assured her. "So let the ranch hands deal with Buck. And we better concentrate on the roundup. We'll have about three dozen hungry cowboys to feed this weekend, not to mention the other family members."

"That's why I'm here." Mallory let herself smile. This was the weekend she came home every year. Lazy K Ranch's late-spring roundup. With Mallory's busy horse broker's business in Levelland, they couldn't get back to Midland very often. Just about four times a year.

"Are you going to make fried chicken?"

Rosalie nodded. "Your dad has already put in his order. He knows it's the only time I let him indulge in fried foods. How about you making that potato casserole?"

"And some red beans and rice, of course." Mallory reached for a note pad when her attention was drawn to the kitchen window. Outside, a horse and rider were walking toward the barn. She looked closer. It was Joe. He was slumped over his mount.

"Rosalie, Joe's back, and something's wrong." She hurried out the door and kept the momentum going until she reached the horse just as two other hands arrived to help him down.

"Looks like he's been worked over," the ranch hand said.

Mallory knelt down beside him on the ground. "Oh, God, Joe, what happened? Where's Ryan and Buck?"

The foreman's face was etched with pain. "Two men ambushed us right before dawn. They shot Buck and worked over Mick and me pretty good."

She gasped. "What about Ryan?"

"That's why Buck sent me for help."

Mallory's heart pounded harder as she looked around for any sign of another horse. "Where's my son?"

"I'm sorry, Mallory." He grimaced. "I tried to stop them, but they took the boy with them."

He had to be overlooking something.

Chase Landon sat in his office at the Ranger Company in Midland, Texas. He'd gone over and over the same information for the past week. He'd prided himself on his ability to find clues that others had missed, but this old case still had him stumped.

Since joining the Texas Rangers nearly nine years ago, one of his goals had been to find his uncle's killer. He also knew he should leave it to the Rangers' Unsolved Crimes Investigation Team in San Antonio. But this was too important to Chase, and he refused to give up.

"Anything new show up?" fellow ranger Jesse Raines asked as he stuck his head though the doorway.

"No." Chase leaned back in his chair. "Ballistics still doesn't match. There had to be another gun there. Another shooter."

"We could go back and take another look." Just being recently commissioned, Jesse was eager to help out on any and all cases. "But after all this time, it's probably long gone."

"I don't think the shooter had enough time to get rid of it," Chase said more to himself than to his partner. He closed the manila folder and stood. "Anything more on the Sweetwater escapees?"

Jesse cocked his thumb toward the door. "The captain is talking with the state troopers now."

Although he'd been in the Midland Company for only the past year, Chase knew this area well. He'd grown up in the oil-rich Permian Basin of West Texas. His first job in law enforcement had been with the highway patrol there.

Suddenly the captain, Bob Robertson, walked in. "Landon. Raines. It looks like we've been called in," he told them. "The two escapees, now identified as Charles Jacobs and Berto Reyes, have shot a civilian and carjacked a vehicle. Now, they've taken an eight-year-old boy hostage. So I need you and your gear ready in thirty minutes."

The captain glanced at Chase. "Sorry, Landon, looks like your vacation is temporarily on hold. I need you on this."

"Not a problem," he said. "Where did they abduct the boy?"

"It was on the Lazy K Ranch. Southeast of Interstate 20."

Chase felt as if he'd been socked in the gut. Then dread washed over him. "Buck Kendrick's place?" He barely got the words out.

The captain nodded. "It's Kendrick's grandson, Ryan Hagan."

Chase stopped breathing. Mallory had a son?

"You know the man?"

Chase managed a nod. "A long time ago." He had trouble thinking of her with a child.

"So you know that even from Kendrick's hospital bed,

he's demanding that every law officer in the state join in the search for his grandson. Not that I blame him." He sighed. "We better get to it. The helicopter will take off in thirty minutes." The captain walked out with Jesse.

Chase sank down into the chair and rubbed his hands over his face. This was crazy.

Mallory Kendrick.

The pretty, ebony-haired girl with big green eyes. An incredible contrast to her olive skin from her mother's Spanish roots. Tall and slender, she had legs that men fantasized about. But Chase had had to quit seeing her. She was too young, and way out of his league.

She was the daughter of rich oilman and rancher, Buck Kendrick, and he was a kid from the poor side of town who would never fit into her lifestyle. But damn, even after all these years, thoughts still lingered of what might have been between them.

Mallory Kendrick…Hagan had made him crazy for years. From the time she'd turned eighteen clear through to their heated summer romance and their breakup when he went off to join the rangers.

Chase leaned back in his chair and closed his eyes. If there had been a woman who could have deterred him from his dream…Mallory was the one.

Funny thing was he'd returned to Midland to see if they could work things out between them, but he quickly learned he was too late. He'd remembered vividly how good old Buck persuaded him to back away when he'd showed up at the door and learned Mallory had gotten married to another man and was on her honeymoon.

Over the several months that followed, he'd tried to

convince himself it was all for the best. It didn't stop his misery. Even concentrating on his new career with the rangers, he managed to let Mallory interrupt his thoughts for a long time. She was the one reason he'd nearly refused the transfer here a year ago. He'd wondered if he might run into her. He hadn't so far.

And now, he was going to drive up to her door.

Her son was in danger. That had nothing to do with their past. It was the little boy he had to concentrate on…the boy he had to find. As a ranger, he couldn't walk away.

Mallory stayed in the kitchen, and there was no point looking outside to see anything. It was after dark, and in the country that meant black as pitch. Besides, there were dozens of law officers who had cordoned off the area and set up a base at the barn. She could go down there. And do what? What she wanted was to grab one of Buck's guns, climb on a horse and go search for her child. They weren't about to let her do that. Look where that had gotten Joe and Buck.

She had seen her father brought in hours ago. She didn't go with him in the ambulance, sending Rosalie instead. Luckily, his wound wasn't life threatening, and he only had to spend overnight in the hospital.

Afraid and anxious, Mallory resumed her pacing while her mind worked overtime thinking about how scared Ryan had to be. And she knew that the convicts were lifers and had nothing to lose if they killed her son.

No. No. A tear ran down her face as she began to tremble again. She had to get him back. Ryan was her life…. They'd gone through so much together.

Her thoughts turned to the man from her past. Chase Landon. Nine years since Mallory had seen him. Back then he'd been a state trooper, with dreams of being a Texas Ranger. And when that day finally came, their idyllic summer had come to an end...and he had walked away from her, breaking her young heart.

Now, that man was going to be the one to help rescue her son. A few years back she'd read the story about how Ranger Chase Landon had tracked a robbery suspect to the Mexican border and talked him into surrendering. She was hoping for the same outcome now.

Hearing the helicopter fly overhead, she felt her heart race in anticipation. More commotion outside, along with voices. She released a slow breath, went to the door and opened it.

Chase stood well over six feet tall. His dark brown eyes were piercing, and his chiseled jaw was rigid. Dressed in army fatigues and sporting a baseball cap, he looked more like a soldier than a Texas Ranger.

Mallory knew one thing. The man still affected her in the same way he always had. His dark brooding looks still demanded respect. She once knew the softer, gentler side of this man, too. Right now, that seemed like a lifetime ago.

"Mallory," he said with a nod.

"Chase. I've been expecting you." She stepped aside allowing him inside followed by another ranger. He was about the same age as Chase, but with lighter hair and coloring. He was nearly as tall.

Chase thought he could handle their meeting after all these years, but seeing Mallory again drove all logic from his head. If anything, she was even more beautiful at almost thirty than at twenty-one. Her midnight-black hair was still long and silky as the wavy strands lay against her shoulders. Her wide green eyes were no longer bright, but frightened, bringing him back to the reason he was here. It didn't stop the strong urge to pull her into his arms. He resisted it.

"Mallory, this is Sergeant Raines, Jesse. Jesse, Mallory…Hagan."

She took his outstretched hand. "It's nice to meet you, sergeant."

He nodded. "Wish it was under better circumstances."

She bit down on her trembling lip. "Just bring my son back to me."

"We're going to try really hard to accomplish that, ma'am." Jesse looked at Chase. "I'll head down to the command post."

"I'll be there soon." Chase had given Jesse a brief summery about his past relationship with Mallory on the trip here. He knew Raines would keep the news private.

They both watched him walk out the door, then Mallory turned to Chase. "You should go, too."

"I will, but first I need to talk with you. How is your father doing?" he asked as he directed her to the kitchen table and pulled out a chair for her to sit down.

"He's going to recover," she said. "He'll be home tomorrow."

"Good. Now, maybe you can answer a few questions."

She looked up at him with those trusting green eyes. He quickly glanced away as he pulled a paper out of his pocket. It was a map of the ranch.

"Joe told us your father made camp here at this group of rocks." He circled the area with his finger. "Right before dawn, two men appeared, one with a gun, catching Buck, Joe and Mick by surprise still in their sleeping bags. Then the convicts took some extra clothes, and the horses. When they went to take your son…Ryan, Buck tried to fight them. He got shot, and Joe and Mick were beaten."

She nodded. "Dad said Ryan wasn't hurt when they took him. Joe's horse wandered back to camp—that's how he was able to come for help." She blinked at tears. "Please, you've got to get my son back before they do anything bad to him."

Chase wanted to promise her he could, but there weren't any guarantees when it came to finding prisoners who had nothing to lose. "We're going to do everything we can to find them, Mallory. They took your father's cell phone, so we're hoping to be able to make contact with them."

"Do you think they're heading to the border?"

"It's a possibility," he told her. "The convicts didn't plan this escape. From the second they'd carjacked the vehicle on the interstate until now being on horseback, I'm thinking that they're just making it up as they go along."

She shivered. "That's what scares me. They're desperate men, Chase. They could just decide there's no need for Ryan any more."

He reached for her hand, a natural reflex. It was cold and shaking as he cupped it in his. "No, Mallory, they *do* need the boy now. He's their bartering tool. So you have to stay positive." He worked up a smile. "I have a feeling Buck taught his grandson how to survive out there."

She nodded, and surprisingly returned with a hint of smile.

It immediately took his breath. Finding his voice, he asked, "Tell me what Ryan knows, Mal."

She released a long breath. "He's a good rider." Her brow wrinkled in concentration. "And can read animal tracks. Dad taught him to how find a direction by the sun and the stars."

"That's good…the boy knows how to handle himself." Chase didn't want to think about the other dangers out there…mostly human ones.

"So you think that could help him?"

He nodded. A strange feeling came over him as he studied Mallory. The woman he'd once cared about… she'd always wanted a husband and family. He couldn't give her that all those years ago. Hopefully he could at least bring her son home.

"He sounds like a great kid."

"He is, but he's still my baby."

He watched a tear fall and he reached out and brushed it away. He couldn't imagine how she felt, but he did feel for her. It was something that hadn't changed. "Mallory, I promise to do everything I can to bring him back."

Chase stood. He needed to put some space between him and her. "I'll be heading out to the camp. If the search dogs picked up their scent we'll follow." He looked around to see the room empty. "You shouldn't be alone. Is there someone to stay with you?"

She shook her head. "No. I sent Rosalie to bed."

"What about your…husband?" Why wasn't the man there with his wife?

She looked at him a long time, then said, "Alan died two years ago. It's just Ryan and me."

CHAPTER TWO

As the sun rose in the sky from the east, Chase knew that the twenty-four-hour mark had come and gone, and they hadn't found them.

He swung his leg over the back of the horse and climbed down, as the other rangers did the same. The bloodhounds were taking a break, too, from their long trek across the dry plains, crossing Interstate 10 into Reeves County. Their trainers had them drinking water beside one of the prison vehicles.

Chase concentrated on his job and knelt to examine the tracks in the sandy soil. There were two sets of hooves and they were headed south. Mexico.

It didn't take a rocket scientist to come up with that equation. Once they crossed the border the two men could get lost for a long time, especially when Jacobs and Reyes had been sent to prison under the "three strikes you're out" law. They had nothing to lose.

And that was what worried Chase the most.

The two weren't taking the easiest route. They were heading toward the Barrilla Mountains. There were fewer towns and traveled roads, but mostly because the rocky terrain provided better cover from the search helicopters.

Still, the escapees had to get across the Rio Grande. That was his job. To make sure they didn't make it to the border, or they might never find them…or the boy.

How could he go back and face Mallory with that kind of news? He recalled the devastated look on her face. It had affected him more than it should have, especially when he needed to keep this case on a professional level.

Hell, how was he supposed to do that when he knew if he'd hung around years ago, so many things might have turned out differently.

Chase took the small picture of the boy, Ryan, out of his pocket and studied it again. His chest tightened as the cute kid with his curly dark hair and big eyes grinned back at him. Envy and regret surged through him as if he were on a runaway horse.

He shook it away as Raines came up beside him. "Same tracks?"

"Looks like we're headed for the border." He slipped the photo back in his pocket, then reached for his cell phone and called headquarters.

Bob Robertson came on the line. "Tell me you located them, Landon."

"Sorry, not yet, Captain. We've picked up their tracks again." He gave their location. "And as we thought, they're headed for the mountains."

"Damn, I wish I wasn't right on that one. Maybe they aren't as dumb as we thought. Do you need more manpower?"

"No, we have enough to handle it." Chase hesitated, then asked, "How is Mrs. Hagan holding up?"

"She's scared, of course," the captain said. "I was hoping to give her some good news."

Chase had hoped that, too. Suddenly he heard Mallory's voice in the background.

"Hold on, Chase. Mrs. Hagan has something to tell you."

"Chase…" She said his name like a plea.

"Mallory, we haven't found them yet."

"I know. It's just that when you do, make sure you tell Ryan that Buck is okay." He heard the tears in her voice. It killed him. "Dad's worried because Ryan saw him get shot."

"I'll be sure to tell him."

There was a long pause, then she said, "Ryan will trust you because you're a ranger."

"Mallory, I'm going to do everything I can to bring him back to you. You got my word on that."

"I know you will. Thank you, Chase."

When the line went dead, he was glad. He needed to concentrate on finding the suspects and forget the past. He clipped the phone back on his belt as Jesse watched him.

"This job is harder when a kid's involved—and especially when it's someone you know."

Chase nodded. Although he'd given Jesse the brief rundown of his past with Mallory, Chase didn't want to delve any deeper. What he couldn't understand was why after all this time Mallory could still get to him.

"It's okay to admit you have feelings for her," Jesse said. "She's a beautiful woman."

Chase glared at him. "This isn't the time to notice a woman. We've got a little boy to find." He thought back to the choices he'd made in favor of his career. Being a Texas Ranger had been all he'd ever wanted. Mallory had been the only woman he'd even thought about sharing a life with. In the end, he chose the career over her. He tried to tell himself she'd been too young for him. Too late he realized that she was everything he'd wanted, but it was Mallory who didn't think he'd been worth waiting for.

She'd married another man.

Chase quickly wiped away that thought as he took a drink of water from his canteen. Too many years had passed to renew a relationship that had been doomed from the start.

"We need to get moving." He walked around his horse, then climbed on and adjusted his hat as Jesse followed suit.

He'd recalled earlier that day when he glanced toward the house and saw Mallory. She tried to look hopeful, brave, but he could see her pain…her misery. Who could blame her? Her child was out there.

He rode off, praying today was the last one they had to spend in this West Texas heat. More importantly, that a little boy would be found safe and could go home to his mother. And Chase could go back to business as usual.

Or could he?

"Stop smothering me, woman," Buck Kendrick growled at Rosalie. "I can walk just fine."

"You're supposed to take it easy so you won't open

the wound," the housekeeper told him as she followed him into the kitchen.

Mallory watched her father's slow gait. He suddenly looked old and he wasn't even sixty yet. He had thick, gray hair, and warm hazel eyes. He was tall and trim, but right now, his broad shoulders were a little slumped over. His expression was pained, and she knew it wasn't from the gunshot wound he'd received in his side.

"Any news?" he asked.

"No. I did talk to Chase Landon."

Her dad didn't look surprised at the mention of Chase's name. "We've got the rangers looking for the boy, we can't ask for anything more."

"You both need to eat," Rosalie interrupted the silence and began to put together the fixings for lunch.

Her father frowned. "Crazy woman. She thinks about food at a time like this."

"Rosalie is trying to stay busy the best she can."

Buck cursed. "I should be out there looking, too."

Mallory felt the same way. "No, Dad. Let the rangers do their job. Like you said, they're the best. And they're trained for this kind of thing."

"I know. I know." He sank into the kitchen chair. "I shouldn't have let them take Ryan…. He's so little. I begged them to take me instead."

Even though Buck wouldn't normally have begged any man, he would have for his family…his only grandson. He loved the boy more than his own life.

Mallory sat down beside him. "I know you did, Dad. None of this is your fault."

"Damn. What kind of world is it when you aren't even safe on your own land? They stole my grandson."

Mallory remained silent and let her father vent. This was a second time Buck Kendrick hadn't been able to protect his family from the cruelty of the world.

He finally looked at her. "Have you told Landon about Ryan?"

Although they'd never openly talked about it, her father knew about Ryan and she'd wondered when this day would come. She shook her head. "No. But he'll know soon enough."

Buck nodded in agreement. "Whether he figures it out himself or not, it's time he knows the truth. And Ryan, too."

Nearly three hours later, the search team finally lucked out.

A local rancher gave them the information they'd been hoping for. Two men and a boy on horseback rode along the back of his property, heading toward the foothills. The rancher also told them about a line shack at the base.

"If the rancher hadn't spotted them," Jesse began, "the shack could have made a perfect hideout."

Chase nodded. "And there's some supplies there. Even if they just stop for some food, we've gained some time."

"They still have about an hour on us."

Chase discussed the situation with the other men. They decided to keep the dogs at the ranch house. And Chase and Jesse would ride up alone, hoping to catch the escapees off-guard. After the rancher gave them directions for a back route to the cabin, Chase and Jesse headed through the rough terrain of the mountain range, using the thick trees for natural cover. The jeep, with backup men, waited about a mile way. Chase hoped the surprise element worked. They didn't need to put Ryan in any more danger. If they weren't careful, this operation could go bad real fast.

At a group of rocks behind the rough-hewn cabin, they climbed off their horses and tied them to a tree. Silently, they made their way toward the back of the structure, happy there weren't any windows. Once flattened against the structure, Chase crept along one side as Jesse moved along the other side toward the open front door. He listened to the voices inside.

"We can't stay the night," one of the escapees said. "We can't even stay another hour. I tell you they're on our trail."

"The kid's asleep in the saddle," the other man said. "And I'm tired of carrying him. Besides, the horses aren't going to last much longer."

"Then we'll take fresh ones from that rancher. There were several out in the pasture."

Suddenly one of the men came outside, wearing jeans that were too short, and an open shirt revealing a once-white T-shirt. Charlie Jacobs. As far as Chase could see he didn't have a weapon on him.

"I'm going to get us some fresh mounts," he called over his shoulder as he jumped down the step and walked to his horse.

Chase made his way to the back of the cabin as did Jesse. He motioned for Jesse to go after the man.

The ranger nodded, then hurried off toward his horse.

Chase went back to the side of the shack. He couldn't see inside to tell where the boy was. And he didn't want to take a chance on rushing in if one of the escapees had a gun pointed at the kid. He had to wait him out.

Ten minutes later, he got a text message from Jesse. *Got him.*

Chase knew Jesse would return as backup. Should he wait? Suddenly there was more commotion inside and the prisoner came to the door. "Stay where you are, *niño,* I need to pee, but I'll be close by."

Chase's heart rate accelerated as the man he recognized in the picture stepped off the stoop and started for the outhouse. He wouldn't get a better chance than this.

Chase took off running and tackled the guy to the ground with a thud. He knocked the air from his lungs, but the man was still able to put up a fight. Finally Chase landed a punch that connected with the man's jaw and threw him to the ground again. Enough time for Chase to pull his gun and aim it at the suspect.

"Go ahead. Give me a reason to shoot you…dead."

In answer Reyes cursed in Spanish, and raised his hands over his head. Chase instructed him to get into position, then he pulled his handcuffs off his belt and put them on him.

About that time, Jesse showed up. He grinned. "Sweet mercy. This is turning out to be a good day. Really good day."

Chase wasn't sure about anything until he saw the boy and knew he was safe. Once Jesse took charge of the prisoner, Chase holstered his gun and took off toward the shack. At the doorway he stopped, not wanting to frighten the boy.

"Ryan," he called out. "Ryan, it's okay. I'm a Texas Ranger."

He looked inside to find a small figure huddled in the corner of the bunk. His eyes were big and red from crying. Chase blinked in the dim light and studied the boy's dirty face, but he recognized him from the picture.

"Are you gonna take me home to my mom?"

Chase allowed himself to smile. "Yes, I am. She said to tell you that your grandpa is okay."

Ryan's eyes brightened. "Grandpa tried to fight them. I'm glad he's okay."

The kid had dark eyes and curly brown hair. His face was long and there was a small cleft in his chin. His features were so unlike Mallory's, but he looked familiar.

"Are you really a Texas Ranger?" Ryan said, interrupting his thoughts.

Chase nodded as he pointed to the silver badge on his camouflage shirt. "Yes, I am. We've been tracking you for miles. Boy, is your mom going to be happy to see you."

With a smile the boy climbed off the bed and came to Chase. "I bet she cried 'cause I got kidnapped."

Chase knelt down in front of the boy. "She's been pretty brave, too. You're very important to her and your grandpa."

Chase felt something tighten in his chest. What if they hadn't got here in time?

"Did they hurt you?" Chase asked.

Ryan shook his head. "Not much. They pulled me around some. But I didn't cry," he said as he pulled up his shirt to show off some bruises and red welts along the thin torso.

Chase examined him and was drawn to a strawberry-colored birthmark on his small chest. It was very similar to the one Chase had on his lower back. The same type that his Uncle Wade had on his shoulder.

Chase stood, but his gaze remained on the boy. His lungs didn't seem to work as he noticed so much more about the child. The similar chin with a small indentation. His dark eyes…

He shook his head. He couldn't think that Mallory would do this to him. Nothing this cruel.

"Are you taking me home?" Ryan asked.

"Yes, so we need to get going."

It surprised Chase when the boy slipped his small hand into his. "I'm ready." Together they walked out to the porch to see Jesse come toward them.

"Boyd and Grant have the prisoners secured…." A slow grin appeared as he studied the two of them. "If I didn't know better I'd say you two looked like—" He paused. "Sweet mercy," he breathed as his smile died away.

"Close your mouth, Raines. We need to get the boy back to his family."

Jesse nodded. "Right. Then you bring…Ryan down by horseback. And the helicopter is going to meet us at the ranch."

Chase nodded. He didn't want to speak right now. What could he say? Until he confronted Mallory, he wouldn't know for sure. He stole another glance at the boy.

That wasn't true. There was no doubt in his mind that Ryan Hagan was his son.

* * *

Hearing the helicopter overhead, Mallory hurried outside. It had been two hours since Chase's phone call and she'd heard Ryan's voice. Her son was back safe.

They landed about a hundred yards away in the pasture, but she didn't care. She took off running. She needed to hold her child in her arms, to see for herself he was safe.

The blades were slowing down as Chase stepped out, then reached back and lifted Ryan to the ground. Together they started toward her. Father and son.

She stumbled on seeing the two together. They were so much alike, everyone had to see they were related. As much as she dreaded this day, she was happy it was finally here. The only problem was how much Chase and Ryan would hate her for keeping this secret?

"Mom," Ryan called and shot off. He nearly jumped into her arms.

"Oh, Ryan," she cried. "You're safe." She hugged him tighter. Inhaled that wonderful familiar boy's smell of dirt and sweat. She loved it. She released him and did a quick examination. Although he'd been checked out in a small clinic near where he'd been found, she needed to see for herself. "You sure you're okay?"

His head bobbed up and down. "I'm okay. The doctor said I just got some bruises." He yanked up his shirt. "But they don't hurt anymore."

Just then Buck and Rosalie appeared and were calling to him. Before Mallory could stop her son, he shot off toward them. She was left alone with Chase. She finally was brave enough to look at him.

"Is he mine, Mallory? Is Ryan my son?"

Mallory swallowed and managed a nod.

His jaw worked. "We need to talk." He glanced toward Ryan. "I'll be back tonight."

"No, it's too soon."

He tipped his hat back, his gaze bore into hers. "Too soon? Hell, Mallory, I'd say it's years too late."

He turned and walked back to the helicopter. The pilot started it up and soon it was in the air.

What was she going to do now? How could she explain everything away?

Buck waited for her as Rosalie took Ryan on ahead into the house. "He's going to take a bath."

She shook her head. "Kids are so resilient, aren't they?"

"Oh, I think Ryan's going to have his share of nightmares for a while." He studied his daughter. "But we'll be here for him."

She felt the tears sting. "Chase knows, Dad. He knows Ryan is his son."

He nodded. "It's time. That boy needs a father…a real father, but only if Chase will be there for the boy."

Mallory didn't need to go into the reasons for their breakup. Buck Kendrick hadn't been happy about his young innocent daughter dating a man who never planned to make a commitment.

"I've made a lot of mistakes, Dad. To start with, I never should have married Alan…. I should have tried harder to contact Chase."

"Sweetheart, we can't stand here and try to atone for all the mistakes made in our lives. If so, I'd have to take some blame, too. I pushed you into that sham of a marriage…but you and Alan seemed to be a great match." He shook his head. "I had no idea that would turn out so badly."

"Dad, stop it. It was my choice."

Alan had been her boyfriend in high school, but knew his feelings for her were stronger than hers for him. When Mallory went off to college she ended their relationship, knowing she wanted to experience life. But they'd stayed friends. When she came home that summer from college and saw Chase, she fell hopelessly in love.

Chase didn't. When he got the call to join the rangers, he was packed and gone without so much as a backward glance. Alan had been the one who came back into her life and was willing to take on another man's baby. So she thought…

"But he hurt you and Ryan…and I can't forgive him or myself for that."

"Maybe if I'd tried harder to contact Chase all those years ago, it would have made a difference." She looked toward the house. "Now, my only concern is protecting my son."

He had a son…. He had a son….

The rest of the day those words had played in Chase's head, even during all the paperwork and debriefing on today's capture. He'd thought it would keep his mind off facing Mallory's betrayal. It didn't do any good. He was angry. How could she keep their son a secret?

Jesse stopped by his office right before the shift ended. "Hey, Chase. Wanted to let you know that Jacobs and Reyes are back in Sweetwater." He shook his head. "Man, I'm glad they're in lockdown now, especially

Jacobs. He's one mean son of a gun. The guy seemed to get pleasure out of telling me what his plans were for the boy. Reyes was pretty talkative, too. He was interested in your relationship to Wade Landon."

That wasn't uncommon. "How so?"

Jesse shrugged. "When I said Wade Landon was your uncle the guy just grinned. Think he'd know anything?"

"What's Reyes? Forty-two? He could have been around back then. I guess it wouldn't hurt to check his record…. Monday." Reyes wasn't going anywhere.

Jesse started to leave, then turned back. "You want to go for some food…maybe a beer?"

"Thanks, but I have plans," Chase told him as he cleared off his desk.

Jesse didn't move. "Well, if you want to talk, I'm around," he said and started to leave.

"I'm going to the ranch to talk with Mallory."

Jesse nodded. "I'd say that's a good place to start." He smiled. "Well, like I said, I'll be around if you want to…get a beer."

"Thanks."

Chase watched as Jesse walked out. Would he ever be ready to talk about this? If he were honest, he wasn't sure about his own feelings. How are you supposed to handle the news that you're a father? That you have a son? There were eight years he'd missed with his boy. How was he supposed to feel? The problem was he felt too many things, joy…fear…and a lot of anger…

Before seven that evening, Chase had showered and changed, then walked out of his town house and climbed into his dusty white truck to head to the Lazy K Ranch.

He knew one thing. Learning Ryan was his kid had affected him like nothing else had in his life. He'd spent less than two hours with the child, but already he felt a bond.

But an instant father? What if Ryan hated the idea?

Chase turned off the highway and drove down the road that led to the Lazy K Ranch. He'd traveled this route many times when he'd been dating Mallory. Mostly he'd come by when Buck wasn't home or out on the range. Her father hadn't been crazy about a—so-called—older man dating his college age daughter.

Chase made a snorting sound. He was all of twenty-eight back then.

His heart rate accelerated as he pulled into the circular drive of the Spanish-style home. The golden stucco-and-stone structure revealed Buck's wife, Pilar Kendrick's, Spanish heritage. The patio out front was made of hand-painted tiles with a large fountain in the center. He climbed out of his truck and went to the door and knocked.

It wasn't too long before he heard footsteps from inside. "I'll get it," called a child's voice. The door opened and a freshly bathed Ryan with his hair combed neatly stood smiling up at him.

"Hi, Chase."

"Hi…Ryan," he answered, suddenly feeling awkward.

"Mom said you were coming tonight. Will you have supper with us? Rosalie made enchiladas."

"That's pretty hard to pass up."

"It's my favorite." His dark eyes were bright. "That's why she made it. For me."

Chase stepped though the doorway into the terra-cotta tiled entry with rough-plastered, cream walls and dark wood trim that matched the rest of the house.

"You should get special treatment," he told him. "You were brave to handle everything."

"And I didn't cry…much," he said proudly, then leaned forward. "I got scared sometimes, but don't tell Mom 'cause she'll start crying again, and I don't like it when she's sad."

"It's our secret."

"What's your secret?"

Chase looked toward the archway that led into the living room to find Mallory. His chest constricted as if he couldn't draw air into his lungs. She had on a long, multicolored skirt and a rose-colored T-shirt. Her shiny ebony hair lay in soft waves against her shoulders. Although her green eyes were weary, she looked beautiful. That was something he didn't need to notice tonight…or any night.

"Nothing. Just some guy talk."

"Well, you can talk about it later. Rosalie says supper is ready." She looked at Chase. "I hope you're hungry."

He nodded as Ryan ran on ahead. "This isn't going to keep us from having our discussion."

"I know, but Ryan needs family right now." She straightened. "This doesn't just involve the two of us, there's a child to think about. And I'm going to do everything I can to protect him."

"Is that what you've been doing for these years, protecting him from me?"

"However you feel about me, Chase, don't take it out on Ryan. We'll settle things after my son goes to bed."

"I agree with you there, except he's *our* son, Mallory." He glared at her. "You need to remember that from now on."

Mallory sat on Ryan's bed watching him sleep. She silently thanked God over and over again for bringing her son home safely. When he'd been kidnapped she wasn't sure she'd ever get the chance to put him to bed again. Now that she had a second chance, she also had a second threat. Was Chase a threat to her family?

She saw the look on his face during supper, and knew he wasn't just going to walk away. And she wouldn't deny Ryan his father, either. Not again.

She placed a kiss on her son's forehead and watched as he curled up on his side and snuggled deep into the pillow. She walked out and closed the door behind her.

Whatever was going to happen with Chase, she still had to return home to Levelland in a few days. The success of her business depended on her being there. She couldn't expect her partner, Liz Mooney, to handle both the training and the broker business. She headed down the stairs to the great room where she had left Chase with her father.

Surprisingly, she found the two men leaning over the dining table going through one of Ryan's baby albums. She hadn't wanted to notice how devastatingly handsome Chase was. At nearly thirty-seven, he was toned and trim. She sighed as her gaze roamed over his long body. He wore jeans better than any man she ever knew. They rode low and fitted over his tight rear end and muscular thighs.

"That's the first time I got him on a horse," Buck said. "Mallory threw a fit."

She started into the room. "That's because Ryan was nine months old."

"I was holding him…firmly," her father said.

She frownéd at him. "He was still too young to be on a horse."

"After that she wouldn't let me take him out of the house until he was three."

Mallory smiled, but Chase didn't. She didn't blame him. She'd been the one who'd caused him to miss all those years.

Buck closed the album. "Well, I think I better call it a night." He turned to Chase. "I can finally sleep now. Thanks for bringing Ryan home."

Chase nodded. "I'm glad it worked out."

Buck paused for a long time. "So am I." He placed a kiss on his daughter's cheek and walked out of the room.

Mallory suddenly felt nervous. For a lot of years she'd wondered about Chase. She'd known he'd become a Texas Ranger, but she never dreamed he'd be back here…in this house.

And after today everything would change…her life and Ryan's life would never be the same.

"Can I get you some coffee?"

"No," he said as he folded his arms over his chest. "All I want right now are some answers."

She nodded, directed him to a brown sofa, and took

the chair across from him, putting the glass-top coffee table between them. "Ask whatever you want."

"I'll start with the obvious. Why didn't you tell me you were pregnant?"

"At first, I couldn't believe it was true," she said weakly. "We used protection."

He didn't respond.

"And I *did* try to call you."

"Like hell you did," said growled. "I don't remember any phone calls from you saying you were pregnant with my child."

She took a breath and let it out. "I called…your mother. I asked her to get you a message…and that it was important that I talk to you."

She saw a glint in his eyes that told her he'd gotten the message. "You should have tried harder— Told her the reason."

"The day we broke up and you left, I was devastated."

"If I remember correctly, you were the one who told me to get out," he challenged.

Mallory remembered everything about that last night. They'd made love. She told him she loved him…and he told her he was leaving for Austin to join the rangers. "You chose to leave."

"I told you before we started dating, that our relationship couldn't go beyond the summer because I would be leaving for training. Besides, you were returning for college."

"That was my father's plan. I wanted to go with you, and you didn't want me. You let me know that being a Texas Ranger was all you wanted."

His jaw tightened. "So to punish me you didn't tell me about my baby and you married another man."

"It wasn't like that." She stood and went to the window. "I was so hurt. My world ended when you went off to Austin. I was convinced you'd find someone else…and forget all about the naïve college girl back home."

She took a breath, and continued. "About three weeks later, Alan came to the ranch with his father. I hadn't seen him since we graduated high school. We'd dated off and on, but mostly we used to be friends." She looked at Chase's stone-cold glare. "I had just learned I was pregnant… I was shocked and scared. And, yes, I told Alan. He listened to me, let me cry it out. He told me he'd always love me…that he'd take care of me and the baby. He asked me to marry him right then." She left out the part about Buck's trouble with the ranch, and Alan's father stepping in as a business partner.

Chase's fists clenched. "Nice to know you forgot me so quickly."

"I didn't!" she gasped. If he only knew how much she'd loved him. She also didn't tell him she was terrified to be a single mother. "I didn't decide to marry him until after I tried to call you several times, but you never returned those calls." She paused for his explanation. She got none. "You weren't coming back to me, were you?"

His gaze never broke with hers. "Doesn't seem to matter now. You didn't give me the chance."

"It seems answering my phone call would have given you a big chance." She felt tears well. Even after all these years, why did it still hurt so much? Pride was fighting with her emotions. "So when Alan asked me to marry him, I accepted."

"After all these years of your silence—when you've been living happily ever after with my child—you expect me to believe anything you say."

CHAPTER THREE

MALLORY WAS FUMING. How dare he?

"I didn't think you wanted us." She lowered her voice. "You didn't call me, or see if I was okay."

He glared at her for a long time. "So you just hopped into bed with another man to find a more favorable father for your baby."

"No, it wasn't like that. We—" She stopped. There was no reason to tell Chase about how long it took her to give herself to her husband.

"You what, Mallory?" he prodded. "Found it easy to give yourself to another man."

"No, it wasn't easy. You knew you were the first man…and how much I loved you." She took a breath. "It was you who didn't want me… And I was convinced you didn't want our baby, either."

He was silent as he glared at her. "If I'd known we created a child that night, I never would have left you."

She closed her eyes. "I didn't know that. I was young and scared, Chase. And so unsure that I could compete with your dream." She tried to stay calm. "And you had always made it clear that avenging your uncle's death, and being a ranger came first in your life."

Chase's gaze moved from hers, not before she saw a flash of his own guilt, too. So she'd hit a nerve. He wasn't so righteous now.

"Maybe I was wrong to turn to Alan, but he said he loved me…that he'd love Ryan." She hesitated and that caught his attention.

"What happened?" he repeated. "What did Hagan do? Did he change his mind about the boy?"

"Nothing at first, he was a good husband…and good to Ryan. But he wanted more children…."

"But what?" Chase coaxed.

"I agreed, but I never got pregnant and Alan learned he couldn't father a child. After that our marriage was never the same. And his relationship with his son was… strained."

"Stop calling him that," Chase said angrily. "Ryan is my son." His hands clenched. "What I want to know is was the boy punished for your husband's…inadequacy?"

"No! And stop interrogating me like a criminal. Alan never lifted a hand to Ryan." Her husband had saved that for his wife. "We separated not long after that." Her voice softened. "About two years ago Alan was killed in an accident."

"It still doesn't excuse what you did, Mallory. You kept my son from me."

She wasn't about to tell him her recent plans to find him. He wouldn't believe her. "And you ran out on me," she emphasized. "I was miserable and lonely, and I turned to another man who promised to love me. I never got any promises from you."

Chase opened his mouth to argue when a child's cries drew their attention.

"Ryan," Mallory gasped as she ran to the stairs and hurried up to his room. Chase was right on her heels.

She pushed open the door, rushed to the bed and eased down beside her son as he was thrashing around on the mattress. "Ryan, wake up, honey."

The boy gasped and sat up. "Mom!" he cried and hugged her. "They're coming after me again."

"No, honey." She held him close. "Those men are in jail. They can't hurt you anymore."

Chase stood at the door feeling awkward as he watched Mallory rock her son back and forth. This was all so new to him. How do you learn how to be a father? How do you make up all those lost years?

Maybe he should just walk away. Who would know? He saw the boy's tears in the dim light and something tightened around his heart. Ryan had stolen that same heart the second Chase walked into the shack to find the eight-year-old trying to be so brave.

No, he was staying put. "Ryan…" He walked inside and stood at the end of the bed.

"Chase…" Ryan quickly wiped his eyes. "You're still here."

He nodded. "Your mom and I were talking. I wanted to make sure you were okay. Sometimes after something bad happens, people get scared again."

"Grown-ups, too?"

"Yeah, I've seen grown men cry. How you acted the

last two days was very brave. And a lot of people get nightmares." He walked around to the side of the bed and sat down across from Mallory. "I've had a few myself."

"Really?"

"I wouldn't lie to you."

That got a smile from the boy and another funny feeling erupted inside Chase.

"Ryan, you still need to go back to sleep," his mother added. "There's the roundup tomorrow. And if you want to help—"

"I do," he told her, then glanced back at Chase. "Will you come, too? It's so much fun. Grandpa can't ride but I get to help 'cause I'm eight this year."

"Ryan, Chase probably has to work."

"No, as a matter of fact, I'm off for the weekend." He smiled at Ryan. "It's been a few years since I did any roping. Maybe you can show me some pointers."

"Sure. So you'll come?"

"Wouldn't miss it."

Mallory turned back to her son. "You will unless you get some sleep." She kissed him and placed a light-weight blanket over the boy. "Good night, Ryan."

"Good night, Mom. Good night, Chase."

"Good night, son," they both said in unison.

Mallory allowed Chase out first, then she flicked off the light and closed the door. Silently they walked downstairs.

"Are you angry because I said I'd come tomorrow?"

She shrugged. "I'm protective of my son."

"Our son."

She didn't hide her frustration. "Okay, let's discuss

our son. You really want to be in his life?" When he started to speak, she raised her hand. "Before you answer, Chase, be sure, because once you announce you're his father you can't just walk away. I won't let it happen to him, not again…and I don't care if you are a ranger. I'll fight you or anyone to protect that boy."

An hour later, Chase found himself parking his truck in front of Jesse Raines's house. Too keyed up to go home, he decided to take him up on his offer.

He walked to the door, seeing the small tricycle and toys scattered in the yard. Another pang of sadness rushed through him as he knocked, then wondered if he should have just gone for a drink by himself. He wasn't the type of guy who shared much, especially not his feelings.

All that changed when the door opened and Jesse appeared. Dressed in nylon shorts and bare-chested, the young ranger looked as if he'd just finished a five-mile run.

"Hey, what's up?"

"Is it too late to take you up on that offer for a beer?"

Jesse smiled. "Never. Just happen to have a couple cold ones."

Chase stepped inside the neatly kept living room. An overstuffed sofa and chair were placed in front of the large television. Next to it was an overflowing toy box. The sound of kids in the background was muffled by a closed hall door.

Jesse slipped on a T-shirt and motioned for him to follow him into the kitchen. He opened the refrigerator and took out a couple of long neck bottles. When Chase had transferred to Midland, Jesse had been the one who reached out to him. They had become friends.

He twisted off the caps and handed one to Chase. "How'd it go tonight?"

Chase took a long drink, then shrugged. "Ryan was happy to see me."

"That's a good start." Jesse walked to the sofa. "So you're the boy's father?"

Chase nodded and took the chair at the table. "Yet, I don't have any legal right to be with him. Hagan is listed as his father on the birth certificate."

Jesse took a drink. "You can go to court—that is, if you want to acknowledge Ryan."

"If you think I'm going to cut and run—"

"I didn't say that," Jesse interrupted. "But there's being a father, and there's being a father. You can write a check for child support, or you can take an active role in his life."

Chase got up. "Hell, this is all so new to me. It changes everything." He thought about his career plans. "I don't have family anymore. When Mom died a few years ago…" He paused, thinking about Sara Landon who had wanted nothing more than a few grandkids. "Damn, she had a grandson."

"Don't do this, Chase," Jesse warned. "You didn't know about the boy, either."

"And according to Mallory, she tried to contact me. Then this…Alan raced in to rescue her. Later on her marriage went sour…."

"You believe her?"

He paced, recalling years ago his mother calling him

about Mallory's message. He was still angry over the fight, and decided not to talk to her just then. "Yeah, and for Ryan's sake, we need to get along."

He looked toward the doorway and saw the petite woman with blond hair holding a baby in her arms. Jesse's wife, Beth.

"Hi, babe," Jesse said as he went to her. "Do you remember, Chase Landon. Chase, this is Beth, and this sweetie is Lilly." He squeezed the baby in his arms and was rewarded with a giggle and a pat on the cheek. "Our son, Jason, is sleeping."

"Hi, Beth. Sorry to intrude on your family time."

"Please, Chase, you're welcome here any time." She stood next to her husband and he wrapped an arm around her shoulders and pulled her close.

"Jessie told me about your rescue today...and finding your son. You have to be so happy."

Chase glanced at Jesse. There's no doubt he shared the news with his wife. Was that how loving couples did things? "Yeah, I'm very happy he's safe, but under the circumstances of how I learned about him, I'm still working on that."

She nodded. "I'm sure you are."

"Do you have any advice for me?"

"Just think about your son. Put him first."

Yeah, think about Ryan. Anything to keep his mind off beautiful Mallory and how much he'd once loved her. All he had to do was think about her keeping his child from him.

"I need to go." He set his bottle on the counter. "Nice to see you again, Beth. You, too, Lilly."

After the goodbyes, Jesse handed the baby to her mother. "I've been invited back to the Lazy K for their roundup tomorrow," Chase said. "You want to come along?"

"I think I'll pass," Jesse said, following after Chase. "The past two days in the saddle were enough for me." He smiled. "Besides, I wouldn't want to intrude on your father/son time."

Early the next morning, Mallory watched Chase's truck come up the road. Some things never change. When Chase Landon gave his word, he stuck by it. So she knew that if he decided to be in their son's life, he would be there.

And now, that was something she had to deal with from now on. She also had to take the blame for this. It had been a mistake not to tell him about his son.

She'd been a coward back then. She'd married in haste and realized not long after that it had been a mistake. Alan had seen her regret, too, but he wasn't about to let her go, and had used subtle threats to keep her under his thumb. She'd worried mostly about Ryan's safety. She'd stayed, but when Alan's drinking got worse and he started taking swings at her, Mallory found a way to leave.

So she couldn't blame Chase if he hated her. She had been weak back then, but no longer. And she couldn't let a war start up between them. Ryan would see it, too. Her son was loyal to her, so their feud wouldn't sit well with the child.

Chase climbed out of the truck. Well over six feet tall, his buckskin boots only added to his height. He was dressed the part of a cowboy in worn jeans and a chambray shirt. His straw Resistol hat sat low on his head, shielding his dark gaze.

Mallory struggled to take a breath into her starved lungs. Darn, he could still get to her.

Suddenly Ryan went running toward his father. He stopped just short of giving him a hug, but his excitement was obvious. Chase put a hand on his shoulder and together they walked toward the barn.

"They look good together," Rosalie said as she glanced away from her task of chopping vegetables.

"Yeah, they do, but will they get along as father and son?"

The housekeeper shrugged. "Not your choice to make. Although it already looks like Chase Landon is staking his claim." She smiled. "I always liked him."

Mallory blinked. "Since when? You hardly said two words to Chase when I brought him home."

"Wasn't my place," she admitted. "Besides, back then Chase was a lot more man than you could handle."

He was definitely that. "Well, as you've witnessed, it seems I'm lacking when it comes to men."

Rosalie shook her head. "No, Mallory, you had to put up with more than a person should ever have to. Look at you. You were a single mother who fought to protect her son, and build a new life. Now, you run a successful horse broker business."

Mallory smiled. "I guess I have done pretty well." She glanced out the window again. "But I've got a really big problem now."

Rosalie took another look outside. "Oh, I don't know. I wouldn't call that good-looking Texas Ranger a problem. Trouble maybe, but seems to me that's exactly what you need to get your blood going."

This time Mallory laughed. It felt good…at least for now.

Chase watched Mallory come out of the house. She was tall and graceful, not to mention beautiful. Even when he'd first met her years ago, she'd taken his breath away…and stirred his body. Dammit, nothing had changed.

"Good morning, Chase," she said in a soft voice.

"Morning," he replied.

"Mom, Chase is going to ride with me. Grandpa has a horse saddle for him. So we have to go."

Mallory nodded to her son. "Okay. Why don't you go and see if your horses are ready. I need to talk to Chase a minute."

The boy frowned, but he took off, leaving them alone.

"Are you going with us to see how I handle myself?" Chase said.

Mallory looked hurt. "Of course not. I trust you." She let out a tired breath. "Look, Chase, a lot has happened in the past few days. Can't we just try and get through this?"

God, he wanted to hate her. Then he thought back to the young girl who'd done everything to draw his attention. She had no idea she already had, the minute he looked into her green eyes. But that was long ago, and he wasn't the same man now.

"There's no getting through anything, Mallory. I'm going to be around from now on. Soon, Ryan will know that I'm his father."

Chase took off toward the corral, leaving her standing there. What did she expect? He wasn't going to be pushed aside any more. He wanted to be a part of his son's life.

Buck was waiting for him with a saddled mount. "I wanted to be able to ride today especially since Ryan is old enough to take part himself. But at least, you'll be with him."

Chase studied Buck. There'd been a time when the man had threatened to throw him off his property. Now he seemed to be welcoming him with open arms.

"I know Ryan is happy you're okay, Buck. This situation could have turned out badly."

The older man visibly shuddered. "I know. I owe you a lot, Chase."

Chase shook his head. "I was doing my job."

"Is it your job to be here today?"

"I'm here because I was invited by Ryan." He straightened. "If you have a problem with that—"

Buck raised his hand. "No, Chase. I'm being overly protective of my family. I guess I want to know what your intentions are."

"Not to be rude, Buck, but that's between Mallory and me."

The older man nodded. "I know it is. Just don't blame my daughter for everything that happened in the past. We both know I had a lot to do with how things turned out back then. I pushed her hard to marry Alan. If it's any consolation, I'll regret it until the day I die."

Chase recalled the heated discussion he'd had with Buck Kendrick. It took place right in this house, just a week after his daughter's wedding…to Alan Hagan.

Before Chase could say anything, Ryan called to him. He waved back and took the horse's reins from Buck. "Like I said, it's between Mallory and me." He walked off.

It wasn't going to be an easy day for anyone. But when he went toward the corral and saw the smile on Ryan's face, he realized it was all worth it.

The boy stood next to a small painted mare. "This is Mazy," he announced. "She's my horse when I come here. I have my own horse back home. First, I had a pony, Speckles, but last year Mom got me a chestnut gelding. His name is Rusty."

Chase linked his fingers together, Ryan placed his boot inside and Chase boosted the boy up into the saddle.

"Do you have your own horse?"

Chase climbed on his mount. "No, no yet. But I've been looking for a small place of my own where I could keep a few horses."

"Well, you get to ride all the time with the rangers."

Chase smiled. "I wish. Most of my work has me in a car. I do get to go out on training maneuvers so we can practice tracking lost boys."

Ryan grinned. "And you're really good, 'cause you found me."

"We had some help, several other men and a couple of bloodhounds."

Ryan pushed his hat down as they rode out to follow the others. "Well, you found me and you captured one of the bad men."

Guiding the horse through the gate, Chase watched the boy expertly handle his horse. "How did you find out all this?"

"Grandpa and I were reading the paper this morning. And he said you knew Mom when she was young."

"Yeah, I knew your mother long before you were born."

The boy looked thoughtful. "Grandpa also said you're a hero."

His chest puffed out a little when his son called him a hero. "No, I'm not a hero. I'm trained to catch bad guys."

The boy looked thoughtful as they rode through the gate. "Maybe I can be a Texas Ranger when I grow up."

"Sure, but it takes a lot of years of hard work."

Those dark eyes that mirrored his gazed solemnly at him. "Good, because I want to be like you."

Chase had to swallow back the sudden dryness in his throat. His son wanted to be like him.

Three hours later, Rosalie and the other women had worked to set up tables on the shaded patio, knowing once the herd was brought in to the holding pens the men would want food, and plenty of it. Well, lunch was ready.

Mallory had gotten a call from Mick saying the men and herd would arrive shortly. She stepped outside to see a dust cloud followed by the soft sounds of bawling calves. She smiled, realizing she hadn't been as worried about Ryan going out as she thought she would be.

Chase wouldn't let anything happen to him.

She grabbed her camera as she stepped off the wooden deck and walked out to the pens. The sounds grew louder and the dust cloud bigger as she climbed the fence railing to look toward the range of mesquite and patches of grass.

She searched the row of cowboys riding drag behind

the herd. It took awhile but she spotted Chase. Tall and broad, and looking comfortable in the saddle, he had his rope in a lasso ready to chase after any strays. Something churned inside her, as she recalled the first time she'd laid eyes on the man.

Chase had been a Texas state trooper then. He'd pulled her over in her new car and lectured her on her reckless driving. She hadn't remembered a word, only his piercing brown eyes and the way he looked in that uniform.

The rest of the summer, she'd continued to race up and down that section of highway just to have him stop her again. He did. Back then, she'd been the pursuer. Three weeks and two speeding tickets later, he'd agreed to go out with her. From the start it had been intense…so hot…and she'd thought…very real.

Mallory released a breath when she spotted Ryan riding next to Chase. It was so obvious to her that they were father and son.

Ryan looked toward the pens, searching for her. He grinned and waved when he found her. She took a picture. She also got several others of the two of them.

Over the next thirty minutes, Buck stood at the gates and supervised the separating of the mama cows from the calves. When the job was completed, they broke for lunch and the ranch hands and neighbors headed for the patio.

Ryan ran up to Mallory. "Did you see me, Mom?"

"I sure did," she told him. "Looks like you're getting pretty good at this. I guess Grandpa doesn't have anything to worry about when he retires and you take over the Lazy K."

He beamed and squinted up at Chase. "Grandpa is going to leave all this to me some day."

"That's a pretty good deal," Chase said as he pushed back his hat.

Ryan did the same. "Well, it won't be for a long time."

"Good," Chase began, "because you need to finish school first."

The boy wrinkled his nose. "That's what Mom says, and then I have to go to college. Why do I have to do that just for some cattle?"

"You have to learn math to know when someone's trying to cheat you...and how to invest all your money."

"Is that important?" Ryan asked.

"Sure is."

"Do I have to go to college to be a Texas Ranger?"

"Yes, you do. That's just part of it. I was a state trooper for eight years before I could even apply to be a ranger."

His eyes rounded. "Wow. That's a long time."

Chase exchanged a quick glance with Mallory. "You know what's great about being eight years old?"

Ryan shook his head.

"You've got time to think about what you want to be when you grow up. So why don't we get some food, I'm starved."

Ryan laughed. "So am I."

"Go wash up, I'm right behind you," he said and the boy shot off.

"Sounds like you had a productive morning with Ryan."

"Yes, we had a good time." He shook his head. "I had no idea how much a kid could talk. Is that normal?"

She smiled. "It's not usual for him, but he's excited. And not everyone is quiet and brooding like you."

"I don't brood. And I just don't talk unless I have something to say." His dark gaze met hers. "Besides, when we were together, we weren't too interested in talking."

Mallory glanced away, unable to stop the flood of memories. They'd been so hungry for each other, there hadn't been much reason for conversation, unless it was to let each other know their desires. "We never talked. Maybe that was the problem."

He studied her for a moment. "No, Mallory, you keeping Ryan a secret is the problem," he said, then stalked off.

Okay, so this wasn't going to be easy. She was willing to do more penance for her sin, but it was going to be on her terms.

She wasn't that young, naïve girl Chase once knew and left without a second glance. She'd survived far too much to let another man dictate to her.

Mallory walked to the deck and stationed herself behind the table and the group of people lined up for the meal. She put on a smile and took over scooping up rice and beans.

"Well, don't you look pretty today, Ms. Mallory," Lee Preston told her as he held his plate.

She'd known the local rancher all her life. "Why thank you, Lee. I'm glad you could join us today. Dad sure appreciates it."

"He had a rough couple of days. I'm just being neighborly. I don't doubt he'd do the same for me."

She served several other ranchers and Mallory came

to realize how lucky she'd been in her life. West Texas neighbors were the best. Her son and Chase were next in the line.

"Rice and beans?" she asked.

"Yes, please, ma'am," Chase said as he nodded his head.

"What about you, Ryan?"

"I'll have the same, Mom," he said as he mimicked Chase. She scooped up their helpings, feeling a little jealous that she'd been excluded.

They started to walk off, then Chase turned back to her. "Will you be able to join us?"

"Yeah, Mom. Come eat with us."

She nodded. "Okay, save me a place and I'll be there as soon as I can."

Chase walked away, knowing he didn't need the distraction of Mallory. But he had no choice. They all needed to get along for Ryan's sake. He sat down at the end of the table and Ryan took the chair beside him.

"It was fun today," Ryan said.

"Yes, it was. It's been a long time since I've herded cattle."

"You're gonna stay for the branding, aren't you, Chase?" Ryan asked.

"Sure," he told him. "I was hoping to team up with you."

The boy pumped his fist in the air. "All right!"

"Your grandpa asked if I wanted to be a heeler. Want to help?"

"That's cool."

"What's cool?"

Mallory arrived at the table and took the empty seat

across from them. Today, she was wearing a pair of worn jeans that hugged those mile-long legs of hers. Her hair was pulled back into a loose ponytail, and some strands had worked free. Her eyes locked with his and suddenly memories of their summer together came rushing back. How easily he'd gotten lost in their green depths, the husky sound of her voice….

He quickly pushed the memories aside and said, "Buck asked me to help with the branding."

"I'm going to help him, too," Ryan said. "Chase asked me." The boy took a big forkful of beans and ate them.

That got a raised eyebrow from Mallory. "I'm not sure if that's a good idea, Ryan."

"Aw, Mom. Grandpa said I could help him this year, but because he got hurt he can't do it." He put down his fork. "P-please, I want to help Chase."

"I'll watch him closely," Chase assured her. He wouldn't let anything happen to his child. "He'll be the third man on the team so that should make it safe enough." They both knew frightened calves could be unpredictable.

Still she hesitated. "Okay, but don't get too carried away." She turned to Ryan. "And you do exactly what you're told."

The boy bobbed his head up and down. "I will. Oh, boy." A big grin appeared. "Can I go tell Joe?"

His mother looked down at his nearly clean plate. "Finish eating first."

The boy gobbled down the last few bites, then stood up. "I'm done."

"That was fast. But haven't you forgotten something?"

His eyes widened. "Oh, Rosalie's pie. I can bring

you back some, Mom." He smiled sweetly. The kid could be a charmer. With her nod, he turned to Chase. "You want some pie?"

"I wouldn't turn a piece down. Any kind is fine."

The boy shot off, leaving the two alone at the table.

Chase could see Mallory was upset. "You think I should have consulted with you before I asked Ryan?"

"I am his mother. It would have been nice. You know the dangers of a roundup."

It made him angry Mallory thought he couldn't keep their son safe. "So it was okay that for two days I tracked down the boy, then rescued him from criminals, but you don't think I'm capable of keeping him safe during branding."

She blinked. "Of course, I know you will. It's just—"

"It's just that you don't want to share your son." He stood, then leaned down and lowered his voice. "You better get used to it, Mallory, because I'm here and I plan to be a part of Ryan's life. A big part.

"I have a lot of years to make up for."

CHAPTER FOUR

WOULD THE WEEKEND ever end?

Mallory walked toward the branding chute and pens just in time to see Chase and Ryan share a high five after they released the calf's hind legs and the animal scurried away. Another hand opened the gate and sent the steer back to its mama.

"Good job," Chase cheered his son. Ryan smiled, puffing out his chest.

This was the second day of the roundup, and the third day Ryan and Chase had spent together. It was easy to see how attached her son was getting to Chase. She didn't believe it was all hero worship, either. Mallory felt her stomach tighten with guilt. For eight years, she'd denied her a real father and still all she could think about was keeping Ryan to herself. Old habits died hard. She was overly protective for a good reason.

Mallory shivered, recalling Alan's constant anger. The frequent fights...the rages that would eventually turn physical. Her own pride kept her from leaving for a long time, but then she had to survive…and most of all, she had to protect Ryan.

She recalled the last time Alan had taken his brutality out on her. Afterward, he'd left the house, and she'd taken her chance, maybe her last. She'd managed to gather her frightened son and together they'd hiked across their property to find safety at her neighbor Liz Mooney's place.

She'd called her father and he brought her back to Midland. Buck had wanted her stay at the Lazy K but she needed her independence, to make it on her own. In the end, she'd accepted Liz's invitation to become business partners. It still hadn't stopped Alan's threats on her and her son. Her ex-husband had even mentioned Chase.

One thing Mallory knew for sure, no other man would control her or her life ever again. She looked toward Chase. Not even a good-looking Texas Ranger.

She stepped closer to the edge of the pen. The amazing father-and-son team was tackling yet another calf. She smiled, feeling the years of regrets that she hadn't given Ryan this relationship sooner. Of course that posed another question she knew she had to face, telling Ryan of her secret.

"Hey, Mom, did you see us?"

She smiled. "Yes, I've been watching you. You're a great team."

Buck stood in the background, giving praise, too. Even Chase gave his son a rare grin. She studied the man she had tried to put out of her mind over the years. It never worked. Just seeing Ryan grow and look more like his father daily didn't help, either.

She had been so much in love with Chase back then. Now, he was back in her life, hating her for keeping Ryan from him. Would he ever forgive her for being young and foolish?

She put on a smile as the dynamic duo came out of the pen. Both were dressed in jeans, Western shirts, and white straw hats; their leather chaps flapped as they strolled toward her. Good heavens, they even walked alike.

"Grandpa said we should take a break 'cause we've been working so hard."

She held out two bottles of water. "I bet you can use these."

"Sure can. Thanks, Mom."

"Thanks, Mallory," Chase said as he took the chilled bottle. He didn't take his eyes off her as he twisted off the lid and placed the bottle against his mouth. Then he tossed his head back and drank half the bottle.

Mesmerized, she watched the sweat roll down his face and had to stop herself from wiping it away. She quickly glanced away. What was wrong with her? She didn't need any thoughts like that. It would only lead to trouble. She stole a glance at Chase. He was watching her with those dark eyes. A warm shiver slid down her spine. Definitely big trouble.

"Hey, Mom, can we go swimming?"

She turned her attention to her son. "Had enough branding?"

Ryan pushed his hat back off his face. "I'm kinda tired."

"Me, too," Chase admitted. "I'll probably have some mighty sore muscles tomorrow." He rotated those broad shoulders. "It's been awhile since I've branded a steer."

"You looked pretty good to me," she said, then realized how that sounded and quickly added, "but if you'd rather swim…"

Ryan looked up at Chase. "I want to swim, don't you? Grandpa's pool is really neat. It's got a slide and a diving board."

"Man, that's a hard choice. Do I want to wrestle smelly calves, or float around in cool water? What should I choose?"

Ryan started to giggle. "The pool. I'll go get my trunks on. Come on, Grandpa's got a lot of extra suits for people."

"Okay, I'll meet you there," Chase called, then looked at Mallory. "Are you going with us?"

She shook her head. "No, but I'll probably hang around to make sure you kids don't do anything stupid."

He smiled. "So you're going to spoil all the fun."

"It comes with the territory of being a parent. Someone has to act like an adult."

"Mallory…"

"Chase…" They both spoke at the same time.

"You go first," he prompted.

She sighed. "I was going to say that we haven't had much of a chance to talk. And since Ryan and I will be leaving tomorrow—"

He frowned. "Whoa…back up. You better change those plans," he insisted. "You're not taking my son anywhere, not until we have this straightened out."

Later that evening, Chase walked out to the Kendricks' backyard. The pool was empty now, and the wrought-iron gate locked for safety. In another section a large manicured lawn was trimmed with yard lights and colorful flowers. The crickets chirped, keeping him company as he waited for Mallory. She was putting Ryan to bed.

Chase paced the terra-cotta-tiled patio. He was anxious and a little angry. No, a lot angry. It happened every time he thought about the eight years he'd missed with his son. Now, Mallory said, "Here are your two days, sorry but I have to leave and take our son."

No, he wasn't going to let that happen. That meant he needed to do something to stop it…legally. He wanted a life with the boy. He knew what life was like without a father. There was no way he'd allow that to happen to his son. He wanted more. The boy was his only family.

Years ago he'd thought Mallory would be his family. As it turned out, she didn't love him, and he'd been quickly replaced by another man. Worse, she walked away with his son. No more. No matter how much she could still get to him, he wasn't going to let her have her way on this.

He'd contact a lawyer tomorrow.

The French doors opened and Mallory stepped outside. She'd changed out of her jeans before supper into a yellow sundress that exposed her delicate shoulders and the golden hue to her skin. Her hair was down, dancing around her face.

"Sorry it took so long," she said. "I helped Rosalie put some things away." She directed him to a grouping of teak chairs around a table.

He waited for her to sit first, then took the chair across from her. It seemed strange that they'd once been lovers, and had made a child together, yet this felt more like a formal business meeting. Maybe that was a good thing.

"I guess what you want is to discuss how we're going to tell Ryan you're his father."

"How generous of you," he growled, but immediately regretted his words.

"Look, Chase. I've already admitted I was wrong not to tell you. I can't change the past. At least believe me when I say I'm not going to stop you from being in your son's life."

"And you need to understand that I can't fully trust you, Mallory."

She looked hurt. "I accept that. But it's Ryan who's my big concern. I don't want him hurt."

Chase cursed, stood and began to pace. "You don't think he's going to be hurt when he learns you kept him from his father?"

Mallory rose, too. She knew she'd be paying for her mistakes the rest of her life. "Yes, he will be. Alan wasn't the father he should have been."

Chase raised a hand. "I don't want to hear about your dead husband. And don't compare me to him. Ryan is my son."

She sighed. "Yes, he is. But tell me, Chase, how active are you planning to be in his life?"

"Very active. I plan to go to court and get partial custody."

Mallory didn't like to be threatened, but she also

knew Chase had the right to do this. She didn't like that, either. "Please don't, Chase. Can't we work something out between us?"

He frowned. "It's a little late, don't you think? You've kept Ryan from me for so long."

She went to him. "If you want to hurt me, fine. But a court battle would hurt Ryan, too."

How different things would have been if Chase had been around to raise his son. It had been something she'd wished for every day in the last nearly nine years…every day she'd looked at Ryan, saw the likeness and remembered how much she'd loved his father.

Would Chase remember what it had been like, too? Although he'd never said the words to her, she always knew he cared for her.

Mallory studied his rigid jaw and knew how stubborn Chase could be. He wasn't going to give in easily, but she had to try. "You and I can work out visitation," she continued. "And I promise, I'll let you see him whenever you want."

He stared at her for a long time. "My, aren't we suddenly eager to cooperate."

"Yes, I am. I love my son. I'll do whatever it takes to keep him from getting caught in our battle."

His gaze bore into hers; then came the smirk. "If I remember, Mal, you enjoyed those battles between us. You had quite a temper when you didn't get your way. We used to get into some pretty heated…arguments."

She had been spoiled back then. She'd grown up fast after marrying Alan. "I've matured a lot since then. Things are different now."

He glanced over her body and she saw a flicker of awareness in his eyes. "Oh, I don't know, you seemed pretty grown up back then, too."

Mallory couldn't stop the blood from rushing to her face. "I was eager to please. I would have done anything for you."

His gaze lingered on her. "And I would have for you. You could turn me inside out with a look. You had a power over me…" He closed his eyes. "Damn. Why did it have to happen like this…" he said, his breath caressing her face. "I would have dropped everything for you…for my child…."

Move away, she warned herself, but couldn't seem to gather up the resolve.

He leaned forward and brushed his lips against hers. She sucked in air as he eased away. "Damn, you could turn me every way but loose."

She bit her lip to keep from begging him for more, told herself she was just curious, but knew it was more. It had always been more with Chase.

He didn't disappoint her and dipped his head toward her. His mouth captured hers. This time there was no doubt about his intentions as he quickly deepened the kiss. He wanted her. Drawing her to him, he moved his legs apart, fitting her intimately against his body. She was just as eager for him as his tongue slipped in and out of her mouth, tasting her, caressing her.

She whimpered, feeling his hands run over her back, searing her skin. He had her unable to think beyond that wonderful hunger he'd always caused deep inside her. Suddenly he released her. In the dim light she could see a mixture of raw desire and anger in his gaze.

"I guess we never had a problem in that department."

She stiffened. "Well, I'm happy you got to test your theory. But in the future please refrain."

"You're right." He walked away, then back again. "I want time with my son."

"I agree, but I live outside of Lubbock, over a hundred miles away from where you live. It's not like you can drive across town."

"Maybe one of us should relocate."

She stared at him for a long time. "I take it, you mean me."

He shrugged. "You were raised here in Midland and your father lives here."

"I've lived outside of Lubbock for years. Ryan was born there…my business is there. I can't leave."

Chase couldn't leave the rangers, either. A transfer was possible, but it could take years.

He caught a glimpse of the woman he'd kissed sense-less. That wasn't wise. It also wasn't wise to learn that he was still drawn to her. Maybe it was good she lived in another town, except he wanted to be close to his son.

"I don't like the idea of being a weekend dad."

"I have room at the ranch. You could stay there when you visit…for Ryan, of course."

So she still wanted to have everything her way. "So that's your answer. We tell Ryan I'm his father, and then you leave here. I don't think the boy's going to be too crazy about that idea."

"No, that's the reason I think we should *wait* to tell Ryan who you are."

He just stared at her. "You don't think eight years is long enough?"

"Ryan's been through a lot. Let him get used to you. I can see you're building a friendship."

Chase hated that she was right. "So are you willing to stay here so I can spend time with him?"

"I can't, Chase. My business doesn't run itself. I have a scheduled horse auction. I've made a commitment, too. My clients depend on me."

"And I have my job here."

She closed her eyes. "Then we'll have to wait until one of us has some time off."

"I guess that would be me. It just so happens, I have two weeks vacation coming. So it looks like you're going to have a house guest for a while."

The next morning, Mallory finished loading the SUV and was ready to leave for Lubbock…and her home for the past three years. Chase had arrived just moments ago to help share the news with their son…that he was coming to the ranch. As much as Mallory wanted a father for Ryan, she knew however this turned out she would end up the bad guy.

At least she had a reprieve for a few weeks.

"I'm coming, Mom," Ryan called and she could hear his footsteps on the stairs. Her heart pounded harder… faster. She glanced at Chase who stood by the fireplace, eyeing a picture of a much younger Ryan. Another reminder of a time he'd missed with his son.

Ryan hurried into the room. He smiled at his mother, then spotted Chase. "Hey, Chase, what are you doing here?"

"I came to see your mother…and you."

The boy's smile dropped. "To say goodbye?"

"Not exactly," she said. "Last night Chase told me that he's been thinking about buying a horse."

"You know that small ranch property I talked about buying?" With the boy's nod, he continued his half-invented story. "Well, it's up for sale and I put in an offer. And I thought since I had some time off, I'd look at some horses." He glanced at Mallory. "Your mom is going to help me find just the right one."

"Cool. We have a lot of horses at our ranch."

Chase relaxed a little. "And that's where I plan to start my search. Your mom has invited me to come for a visit. Would you mind me hanging around for awhile?"

"No! I mean, I want you to come to the ranch."

Mallory had to turn away as another surge of guilt overtook her. She'd lain awake most of the night, trying to think of a way to explain to her son that she'd lied about his father. She hoped over the next two weeks she could find a way.

Ryan continued to cheer. "Oh, man, I can't wait to tell Bobbie Everett." He looked at Chase. "He's my best friend in the whole world. He's gonna flip when I tell him you're a Texas Ranger, and you rescued me."

Buck walked into the room. "Hey, what's all the racket in here?"

Ryan ran to his grandpa. "Grandpa, Chase is coming to stay with Mom and me for a while."

"That's good. Then you can spend some time together."

"He can meet all my friends."

Chase stood next to Mallory, both watching their excited son. Then he turned to her, his gaze moved over her again. "Are you ready for me as a house guest?"

No! "As long as you remember this arrangement is for Ryan's sake," she reminded him. "Let's not make this personal."

He nodded. "Not to worry, I learned my lesson a long time ago."

Before leaving on vacation, Chase needed to stop by the office and talk to his captain. Mallory asked if she and Ryan could follow so they could thank the men involved in the rescue. He didn't object, but was a little disappointed he couldn't introduce Ryan as his son. But that would happen soon enough.

Inside, the rangers gave Ryan a cheer and applause, deeming him a hero for acting so brave during the kidnapping. The captain awarded the boy with a ranger's baseball cap, then Carol, the administrative assistant, showed him and Mallory around the office.

Chase went into the captain's office to let him know he'd be out of town for awhile. "I'll be just outside of Lubbock. Here is the number I can be reached at if you can't get me on my cell."

"It would have to be quite an emergency before I'd call you back from vacation. You're long overdue, Landon." He eyed Ryan and Mallory outside the glass partition. "Just tell me you aren't looking for a new home with the ranger company in Lubbock."

Chase smiled, thinking about how he could put in for a transfer. "Hardly," he told him. But realistically it wasn't so far-fetched for Chase not to consider it. He'd do pretty much anything to be close to his son.

Robertson nodded. "Good. So go and enjoy your vacation."

"Plan to," Chase said as they walked out.

"One more thing," the captain began. "Have you done any follow-up on the escapees, Reyes and Jacobs?"

"What do you mean?" Chase asked, knowing he'd finished all the paperwork from the capture.

"I'll let Jesse fill you in," Robertson told him.

Chase walked out into the hall and met up with Ryan and Mallory. "I have some work to finish with Jesse."

Mallory nodded. "Then we'll take off. You have my directions?"

"You really are coming?" Ryan asked.

"I'm really coming." Chase tugged on Ryan's new hat, finding he was excited to spend time with his son. "Give me a few hours. I need to stop by my place."

Chase looked at Mallory, finding more confusing feelings. And how dangerous it would be to act on them. There couldn't be a repeat of last night's kiss. "I'll see you later, too."

He watched them both walk out the door, then headed down the hall and into Jesse's office. "Captain said you wanted to see me."

He stood. "Probably not important, but Reyes is making noise since he got out of solitary."

"Like what?"

"Just more of the same. He says he has information about Wade Landon's death. And he wants to make a deal."

"He's a three-time loser," Chase said, not wanting to get his hopes up. "There are no deals."

Jesse shrugged. "I know, but it wouldn't hurt to go talk to Reyes."

"What if it's a load of crap?"

"And what if it isn't?" Jesse countered. "What if Reyes knows what happened that day?"

"Then he's got to have more details than just mentioning Wade Landon's name to get me excited."

Chase was pretty sure of one thing; his uncle's death had been a gang-style killing. And Reyes was connected to the *Bandidos* gang, but so were a lot of other men in prison.

He moved toward the door. "Well, it's going to have to wait, because I'm off to the Mooney Ranch for two weeks."

Jesse grinned and sat down on the edge of his desk. "Ryan mentioned it several times." He lowered his voice. "So, you're going to play dad."

"We haven't told Ryan anything yet. I just want to spend some time with him, hoping he'll get used to me."

"From what I've seen of you together, I'd say you're a perfect match. What does his mother think of this arrangement?"

"I don't think she's crazy about me barging in…but she'd better get used to it. I'm going to be in Ryan's life, whether she likes it or not."

CHAPTER FIVE

LATER THAT DAY, Chase turned his truck onto a narrow road about ten miles outside the small town of Levelland, just west of Lubbock. The large tires dug into the loose gravel surface, kicking tiny rocks upward, causing a pinging sound against the belly of the truck.

He turned and drove under an archway that read, Mooney Ranch, headquarters for Mallory K Horse Broker. Chase saw ahead a compound with several whitewashed structures, along with two huge arenas. The house was a large, two-story clapboard, painted a sunny yellow with white trim.

Chase parked next to a mud-crusted truck imprinted with the ranch's name on the side. He climbed out and looked toward the corral where a woman sat astride a large stallion. He gathered she was Mallory's partner, Liz Mooney. He took a moment to admire the skilled rider as she worked the beautiful chestnut quarter horse through the Western Dressage pattern.

They were magnificent together.

Suddenly he heard a screen door slam and a kid's voice call, "Chase!"

He turned to see Ryan jump off the porch step and break into a run. A German Shepherd mix dog scurried behind him, barking. The boy was fast and a little awkward as he made his way across the yard. Chase resisted catching him in a big hug.

"Hey, kid, haven't seen you in a while," he joked.

"Yeah, like two hours," Ryan said, while the dog nudged at Chase for attention. "Max, sit," Ryan ordered, and the animal obeyed. "How long you going to stay, Chase? Will you go riding with me?"

"Ryan, let's give Chase a chance to catch his breath."

They both turned to see Mallory. She was dressed in her usual jeans and a fitted pink blouse. He had trouble pulling air into his lungs, recalling how much he liked that color on her.

He shook his head. *Don't go there.*

"Hi, Mallory."

"Chase," she returned. "You made it okay."

"You gave good directions."

"Hey, Mom," Ryan called, "Can I show Chase around?"

She raised an eyebrow. "Since Chase is interested in buying a horse, how about I show him around? And you can come along."

"Okay, but don't show him my…project. I want to." Boy and dog ran on ahead toward the barn, leaving his parents behind.

"Like I said before, he's got far too much energy."

"Well, you're about to get a big dose of it so you better get plenty of sleep," she warned. "And now that school's out, you'll have him all day long."

He sighed. "I'm looking forward to it."

She finally smiled. "So is Ryan."

His gut tightened as he watched her. If there was anything that hadn't changed over the years, it was that she could still stir him up. He glanced away. "What project was Ryan talking about?"

"I'll let him tell you."

They started walking toward the barn. "How does your partner feel about me…showing up?"

"Liz? If she doesn't like it, she'll tell you."

He glanced toward the corral and saw the woman in question climb down from the stallion. She handed the reins to a man, then walked out of the arena toward them.

She looked to be in her midfifties, but her trim body and long rust-colored braid made her seem more youthful. As she approached, Chase caught her fresh-scrubbed look, showing off a dusting of freckles across her face.

"So you're the famous Texas Ranger," she said, and looked him over. "I thought you were a giant or something the way the lad described you."

Chase laughed. "Sorry to disappoint you."

She gave him another exaggerated once-over. "Oh, no, I'm not disappointed at all. In fact, I'm grateful to you for bringing Ryan back." She stuck out her hand. "Hello, I'm Liz Mooney."

"Chase Landon." He shook her hand. "It's a pleasure to meet you, Mrs. Mooney. Thank you for letting me stay here."

"It's Liz, and it's not a problem. This is Mallory and Ryan's home, too."

Mallory decided it was time to join the conversation.

"We're partners," she added. "Liz is the breeder and expert trainer. I sell the horses and handle the business end of things."

Liz snorted. "Don't let her whitewash it. If it hadn't been for Mallory's skills, the ranch wouldn't have survived. She's built quite a successful business for both of us."

"We've made a good living," Mallory admitted. "And the arrangement has been perfect for both of us. The best part, I get to stay home with Ryan."

"That's good," Chase said, not giving her any attitude. That surprised her. Maybe they could do this.

A horse whinnied and Liz glanced over her shoulder. "Well, it seems a certain guy is getting impatient. I better go and show him who's in charge." She turned back to Chase. "I'll see you at supper."

"I look forward to it, Liz," he said.

The older woman hurried off toward the corral and Mallory and Chase continued on to the barn.

"She seems nice. How long have you been partners?"

"Officially about two years. We were neighbors first. Alan had inherited his grandparents' ranch—the land borders Liz's property." She stopped, not wanting to go into any detail of her marriage. "When I separated from Alan, Ryan and I came here to stay at first. It was only supposed to be temporary, but Liz had recently lost her husband…and lost her desire to train horses. You can say we kind of helped each other through a rough time." She faced him, not ready to explain how Liz's home had become her and her son's safe haven. "She adores Ryan."

"I'm sure your father would have liked you to come home to Midland."

"Of course, but I wanted to be independent. I wanted to teach the same to Ryan." She sighed as they walked on. "I began by helping list Liz's stock on the Internet, along with advertising her training expertise. She has the reigning champion, Sparks Will Fly, in stud here."

Chase whistled through his teeth.

She continued. "And, yes, I sell his stud services via the Internet, too."

He broke out into a grin. "You're quite the business-woman. I'm impressed."

For some strange reason, she cared what Chase thought. "Liz has been a big help, especially when I branched out and started brokering other horses in the area. It took some time, but we've made a name for ourselves."

"I'd say so. I'm impressed, and a little envious." He glanced around. "You have a nice place here."

"Thank you." That meant a lot to her.

"Growing up in an apartment in town, I always wanted a small ranch."

She didn't know that. "I thought you always wanted to be a ranger."

"That, too. But I plan to retire someday."

"I guess I never thought about you retiring, not until you found—" She paused. "I mean you were so anxious to find the answers to your uncle's shooting. Was his case ever solved?"

He shook his head. "No. There hasn't been any new evidence."

She felt his demeanor change. Even after all this time,

he hadn't seemed to let it go. "I'm sorry, Chase. I wish…"
She didn't know the right words to say. She never had.

He stopped at the barn doors, his dark gaze locked
with hers. "You wish I could find the person who
brutally shot Wade, and stripped him of his badge as if
it were a souvenir?" He paused as if composing himself.
"Yeah, me, too. Me, too. Maybe we'll catch a break
someday…and find the guy."

Before Mallory could say anything more, Ryan
called out and waved for him to come to a stall.

"You better go see what he wants."

Chase started down the aisle, but Mallory stayed
back. She'd already gotten too engrossed in his personal
life. It was hard not to react to the pain she still saw in
his eyes. When they'd met, Wade Landon's death had
been fairly recent, and Chase had been so determined
to find the killer. She hated that he hadn't gotten the
closure he needed.

She watched Chase and Ryan and smiled. She
wanted to give them time alone together, although she
wasn't sure what her son had planned for his father.
Maybe if Chase concentrated on just being Ryan's
father, he'd find what he'd been missing.

She knew he had no family left. There'd only been
his uncle and his mother to start with. And they were
both gone. His own father had bowed out of his life a
long time ago. Ryan was all the family Chase had now.
Hopefully, his son could help fill some of that empti-
ness. Regret rushed through her, recalling it was something she'd never been able to do.

"My, my, my. There's a man who'd be hard to pass up."

Mallory turned to see Liz. "I thought you had a stallion to work."

"Juan put on the wrong bridle." Her friend studied her. "And what are you going to do? Just stand in the background and watch them?"

Liz had been one of the lucky few; she'd been happily married for over thirty years. She knew everything from Mallory's past, including Chase.

"What do you expect me to do? Chase let me know a long time ago that he didn't want me in his life…especially after what I did."

"Well, looks like things have changed. You have something he wants…his son."

"I'm not starting up with him just because of Ryan." She couldn't handle that kind of hurt again, not for any man.

"It seems like a good place to start," Liz told her.

Mallory shook her head, knowing her friend's ability to play matchmaker. "No way. One bad marriage is my limit. I'm not letting any man dictate to me again."

"Did Chase show any signs of that before?"

"No, but neither did Alan."

"Are you kidding? Your ex-husband was selfish all of his life. Of course I put a lot of the blame on his daddy and mama who spoiled him rotten. And when he couldn't have you…he tried to control you."

Mallory allowed Liz to be the expert since his grandparents' ranch bordered her property. She'd known Alan Hagan all his life, the good and the bad.

"Just because they were rich doesn't mean they're better than anyone else."

"Well, Alan is dead now." She recalled the horrible car accident he hadn't survived. "He can't hurt Ryan or me anymore." She glanced toward her son. "And I won't let anyone else hurt us ever again."

"Okay, you handle it your way." Liz shook her head and sighed. "Those two sure look good together."

Mallory noticed it, too. She realized that having Chase here was the right thing to do for her son. She wasn't so sure about herself.

After Ryan went to bed for the night, Chase followed Mallory across the compound to his temporary living quarters. They stepped up onto a small porch of the cottage.

"It's not that large, but I'm sure it will meet your needs," Mallory said as she unlocked the door. "And you'll have more privacy here. Believe me, Ryan can be pretty trying. The kitchen has been stocked with essentials. But we want you to come up to the house for meals."

"I'll be fine, Mallory," Chase assured her.

She opened the door, reached in and flipped on the lights, illuminating the room.

Chase stepped inside behind her. He was impressed as he took in the large room that held a sofa, a chair and a kitchenette with a counter and two stools. Down the hall, he found a newly tiled bath and a small bedroom. He tossed his duffel bag on the bed and returned to the main room.

"At one time this was the foreman's house," she explained. "But we don't have one now. A foreman, I mean. And the ranch hands stay in the bunkhouse. We use this place sometimes for guests and clients."

"It's great," he assured her. "And you've been gracious enough to allow me to stay here."

"No, Chase, I owe you. I took away a lot of time you should have had with Ryan." She looked sad. "So any time you want to be with Ryan…you're welcome to stay here."

He wanted more than just to visit Ryan. He wanted his son to come stay with him in Midland, too. Would Mallory be willing to let him visit? "Do you have time to talk?"

Nodding, she sat in the chair while he took a seat on the sofa. "If this is about telling Ryan who you are—"

He raised a hand. "No. So much has happened to him that I think you're right, we should wait a little while. Of course our son isn't stupid. He'll probably figure it out pretty soon on his own. I'd like to be prepared." He paused a minute, trying to figure out how to approach the next question. "How did Alan really treat Ryan?"

Mallory didn't like to talk about her marriage with anyone, especially not Chase. "Alan was attentive to me during my pregnancy, but afterward, he couldn't seem to get by Ryan's different looks, especially after he found a picture of you." She glanced away. "He got angry, but it was directed at me." Mallory felt herself flinch just thinking about that time with her abusive husband. And more and more, Alan was jealous of the time she'd spend with Ryan.

"And I made sure I kept Ryan away. And I know for pride's sake, Alan wouldn't say anything to him." She'd never let the violence touch her son. "I came to realize that I'd made a mistake, and I took Ryan and we left."

Mallory felt the still raw emotions building. She shook her head trying to shut away the nightmare of her marriage. The months of living in fear. Alan's threats of retaliation after she'd left him. For a long time, she'd worried that he might go after Chase.

She sighed. "It was sad for Ryan because he didn't know why he'd never had his father's love. And I couldn't tell him about you."

Chase's fists clenched, wishing he had Hagan alone for just five minutes. He sure as hell wouldn't show the coward any mercy.

Chase also knew he had to take responsibility…take some of the blame. He should have been there for her…for his son. Instead, Mallory had paid the price.

He crossed to her, crouched in front of her chair. "How bad did things fall apart, Mallory?"

She wouldn't look at him. "It doesn't matter," she insisted. "It's over now. I admit the marriage was a mistake. And there's nothing I can do to change the past." Tears swam in her eyes. "Please, believe me, Chase, if I'd known what a disaster it would have been, I'd never have married Alan. If you would have called me…"

God, he hated seeing her tears, her pain. "I know, Mallory. I was angry, too….When I got the message that you called, I couldn't talk to you. What you wanted I couldn't give then," he lied. He had wanted her. He'd just realized it too late.

She nodded and brushed back her hair. "I'm glad you're going to be in Ryan's life. He needs you. I saw that the minute you two were together." A tear found its way down her cheek. She swiped it away. "Just love him."

He couldn't stand it any more. He reached for her and pulled her close. "I didn't think it would happen so fast, but I already do love him."

She finally broke down and sobbed. He scooped her up in his arms and carried her to the sofa, reveling in the fact she clung to him. Her sweet body pressed against his. Even after all these years, it felt so right.

"I'm sorry, Chase," she whispered. "I've made such a mess out of everything."

"Sssh," he breathed and held her. Damn, she was breaking his heart. "We've both made mistakes, Mal. I have to take some blame, too. If I hadn't left you back then—if I'd stayed—" He wasn't about to tell her that he'd returned only to find she was already married…so all he could do was walk away from her a second time.

It broke his heart.

Mallory raised her head and looked at him, her green eyes luminous. "No. I knew all along how much you wanted to be a ranger. And you are such a good one."

"I was wrong to leave you the way I did," he said. "I wish I could go back and change—"

She placed her finger against his lips to stop his words. "We can't do that, Chase." She gave him a sad smile that made his chest ache. "Please…no more regrets. Let's just look toward the future."

He swallowed and managed to nod. He still had a lot to make up to his son. So things were going to be different from now on. He was going to be in both their lives.

She touched his face and he about lost it. "You're a good man, Chase Landon."

What he was feeling and thinking right now was far from being good. "And you're a good mother." He couldn't resist her any longer and touched his mouth to hers.

"Chase…"

"Quiet, Mal. We've talked enough." He was at the end of his patience. His mouth closed over hers, and he forgot about everything else but the woman in his arms. A whimper escaped her as he deepened the kiss. He parted her lips, and delved inside to taste her. She was just as hungry as her arms went around his neck and she pressed against his chest.

He was quickly getting lost in her scent, her touch, her taste. He wanted more…. Pushing her back on the sofa, he started to stretch out beside her, but she resisted and broke off the kiss. There was fear in her eyes as she pushed him away and sat up. "I can't do this, Chase. I just can't." She stood and went to the door.

He sat there a moment trying to gather some composure. He hated that she still could get to him. "It's okay, Mallory. Although enjoyable, it's far too late for seduction."

She gasped. "You're the one who kissed me," she tossed at him. "I only stayed to talk about Ryan."

"It's hard to turn you down when you're so tempting," he said, trying to cover his own weakness. Her. He definitely hadn't been thinking of Ryan when he had Mallory in his arms. "You were a willing participant in the kiss, too."

She shook her head. "I'm not going to jump into bed with you."

He raised an eyebrow, trying to ignore the leftover feelings. "Seems to me we've always had that kind of reaction toward each other."

Her eyes were pleading. "Reactions or not, I'm not ready for this."

"Okay, but there's no reason to be afraid of me."

She squared her shoulders. "I'm not afraid of you or anyone," she insisted. "I just don't want to get involved with you. I think right now we should concentrate on being Ryan's parents."

"That's fine by me." He motioned for her to leave.

"Okay. Good night," she said and walked out.

Chase watched her hurry toward the house. His body still ached for her. Damn, he hadn't planned for this to happen. He didn't want to desire Mallory again. He'd vowed he wouldn't let her get to him again…. But it was too late. He cared about her, probably always would.

There was a lot more at stake this time. With their history, how were they supposed to keep away from each other?

The next morning brought sunshine and mild temperatures for an early June day. Liz was outside unloading the new mare.

Ryan was dancing around the breakfast table setting out the flatware waiting for Chase to appear. Mallory was anxious about the same thing, but for a different reason. She'd overreacted last night.

It was just a few kisses, though Chase's kisses were

anything but ordinary. She shivered. He might be a good guy, but she didn't trust herself, or any man at this point.

"Chase said he'd be here at seven," Ryan said. "He was going to help me on my project."

Mallory glanced at the kitchen clock. It was only ten after. "If Chase said he'd be here, he'll be here." She set down a plate of eggs and bacon. "Now eat."

"Okay," he groaned and had just picked up his fork when the back door opened and Liz came in, followed by Chase.

"Chase," Ryan called as he jumped up from the table and rushed to greet him.

"Sorry I'm late. I helped Liz unload the mare. She's real pretty. After breakfast we'll go see her."

"Are you going to buy her?" Ryan took him back to the long pine table.

"I wish, but she isn't for sale," he said. "She's here to make a foal."

"You mean Spark's going to cover her," her son said in a matter-of-fact tone.

Mallory bit her lip to keep from smiling. Most ranch kids learned about sex from watching it with the animals. Ryan was no exception.

Liz sat down and joined in. "Yep, I'd say Spark is going to be a daddy again."

"But we never get to keep any of them," Ryan complained.

"That's because your mom and Aunt Liz have to make a living," Chase told him.

"I know." The boy smiled again. "I'm lucky, too,

because I have my own horse, Rusty. What kind of horse do you want?"

Chase shrugged. "Not sure yet. I haven't had much time lately to look."

Mallory came to the table carrying two plates, setting one in front of Chase.

His dark eyes met hers. "Thank you," he said.

She swallowed. "You're welcome," she barely managed to say. She sank into the chair across from him.

He was freshly shaven and his hair was combed back from his high forehead. His brown eyes had golden flecks in them and were fringed with long, black lashes. He grinned and her heart leapt. Good Lord. Get a grip. She couldn't do this for two weeks.

She put on a smile, too, ignoring her pounding heart. "I have a few listings to show you," she began. "If you're interested in any, I'll take you to see them."

"Sounds good."

They ate for a while, and Ryan said, "Chase, are you still going to help me with my project?"

"Yes. But I don't know what that project is." He looked around the table, and both Liz and Mallory shrugged.

The boy glanced at Liz, then his mom. "You have to come with me to see it first."

Chase looked at Mallory. She knew her son had been gathering leftover wood from the repairs to the corral and the stalls over the last few months. She suspected that he wanted to build something.

Definitely a father-and-son project.

* * *

After breakfast, Liz went out to the mare's barn while Ryan disappeared upstairs to finish his chores. Chase sat at the table and looked around the big farm kitchen. There were knotty pine cabinets and cream-colored tile covered the counters. The hardwood floors were scarred, and a few of the boards squeaked. It was a great room.

Mallory stood at the sink finishing the rest of the breakfast dishes. She was ignoring him. He had gotten under her skin last night. She had done the same to him, stirring up memories of their time together. A time he didn't need to think about today, or any day.

He didn't want to think about what she'd gone through in her marriage to Hagan, either. It only made him angrier. She wasn't about to trust anyone right now, and after last night, especially not him. He needed to tread slowly, or keep out of her way.

His gaze moved over her slim figure. The nice curve of her bottom was outlined by her jeans. Suddenly his own jeans were uncomfortable and he shifted in his chair. This wasn't going to be easy.

Mallory came to the table with the coffeepot. Her dark hair was tied back into a ponytail, and a thin row of bangs brushed against her forehead. "Want more?"

His gut tightened again. Definitely. "Only if you join me and we talk."

"Unless it's about Ryan, we've already said everything, Chase."

She was right. He'd be foolish to start up anything with her. He had a job with the rangers to return to, and his home was over a hundred miles away. Then he recalled last night and how she'd felt in his arms, the way her lips felt under his…that had him forgetting all practicalities, and everything that had happened in the past.

He also saw her determined look. "Not a problem," he lied.

She looked relieved. "It's for the best. You're trying to build a relationship with your son."

Suddenly Chase realized that he wanted his son's mother included in some of those plans, too. But she was right. It wasn't possible. "You're right. Ryan has to be my main focus. Although, it would help if you would turn ugly and didn't distract me." When a rosy blush spread across her cheeks, he couldn't stop. "You are one hell of a beautiful woman, Mallory Hagan, but I'll try to control my urges."

"Oh, that makes me feel so much better," she said, trying to act irritated.

"Happy to oblige." Grinning, he leaned back in his chair as she sat down across from him.

"All I care about is that you oblige your son."

A warm feeling spread through him. "I like that."

"What?"

"That you called him my son." He leaned forward and grasped her hand on the table and squeezed it. "I might be angry for not knowing about him, Mallory, but never about the great kid you raised."

"Thank you, that means a lot."

There was a sudden commotion upstairs, then a sound on the stairs warned them Ryan was coming. Mallory pulled her hand away.

"Hey, Mom, I finished making my bed and cleaned

my room," he announced, then turned to his father. "Chase, you ready to go now?"

"Sure," he said and carried his mug to the sink. "We'll see you later."

"Yeah, Mom, later."

Together they went out the back door and walked past the barn about fifty yards to where there was a big tree. The thick trunk was split and two branches angled out about four feet from the ground.

"What do you think?" he asked Chase.

He had no idea what Ryan was talking about. "It's a great tree." He moved underneath and looked up into the oak. "You got plans for it?"

Ryan nodded and went to a bush where an old horse blanket covered a stack of wood. On second look they were wood scraps. "I want to build a tree house. Just for me. But I need help."

Chase pushed his hat back. "I'd say so. It's a big project for one guy."

"I know. Grandpa was supposed to help me but he got too busy, then he got shot." Squinting from the sun, Ryan looked up at him. "So I was wondering if you ever built anything before."

Chase eyed the branches, searching for a good base for the platform. "I've built a few things in my day. In fact, I had a tree house once. My uncle Wade helped me build it."

"Cool. So you know how?"

He wasn't an expert with power tools, but he could put something together. "Yeah, I could help you."

Ryan pumped his fist in the air. "All right. Wait until I tell Bobbie about this."

"Whoa, slow down, Ryan. This needs to be approved by your mother first."

His smile drooped. "Why? She won't let me. She'll just say it's too dangerous."

CHAPTER SIX

"OH, RYAN...it's too dangerous," Mallory said, looking up at the enormous oak tree.

Her son gave his best pout, then looked at Chase. "I told you she'd say that. She thinks I'm still a baby."

Mallory resisted the urge to argue with her son. She'd only end up the bad guy. "We've talked about this, Ryan. You could fall out of the tree and hurt yourself. I thought you were going to build something on the ground."

"Mom..." he whined. "That's no fun. It won't be cool unless it's up there and no one can see me. Like a secret hideout."

Great. How was she supposed to keep an eye on her child if she couldn't find him? "It's still pretty high up."

"Chase will build it real strong...and safe. Right?" Those pleading brown eyes turned to Chase.

"Well...sure," he began his pitch to her. "I'd put four-by-four posts in the ground for support, and build the base about six, seven feet high." He raised his hand over his head, giving her an estimate of the height. Then he had the nerve to smile at her. He was worse than Ryan. "I'll make sure it meets all your standards."

"What does that mean?" Ryan asked.

"Her rules on how we build it." He folded his arms over his chest and his gaze caught hers. "What do you say, Mal?"

"Yeah, Mom, what do you say?" Her son stood next to Chase and mimicked his father's words and actions. She was lost. She couldn't take this away from either one of them.

"Are you sure it will be safe?"

"I'll put in extra braces and a sturdy ladder."

"Okay…I guess you can build it."

Her son launched himself into her arms. "Oh, thanks Mom, I love you." Just as soon as he released her, he hugged Chase. "Thanks, Chase. I'm gonna call Bobbie and tell him." The boy tore off toward the house.

Mallory turned back to Chase. "I hope you know what you've gotten yourself into."

He grinned. "I doubt it, but I do know I'm going to love every minute of it."

"I'm sure you will," she said sternly. "But next time, will you come to me first so we can form a united front?"

"It seems a little unfair to gang up on an unsuspecting kid."

She couldn't think with Chase staring at her. "Oh, do you have a lot to learn."

He stepped closer and lowered his voice almost seductively. "Maybe you could teach me some of the secrets of parenting."

She laughed, hoping to break the mood. It didn't

work. "Foolish man, there are no secrets. You just hope you stay one step ahead of them."

He arched an eyebrow. "With Ryan, I doubt that's possible."

"Now you're getting it. Always expect the unexpected and never think or even mouth the words, *my child would never do that.*"

That caused Chase to grin as he raised his right hand. "I promise. But I want something from you now."

She sobered. "What's that?"

"Keep telling me whenever I do something wrong."

She smiled. "That's a guarantee. Just remember, you can't give Ryan everything he asks for."

"It's hard not to."

"I know. And the tree house is a good thing since you two will be working on it together. He needs the company of a man. I'm afraid with just Liz and me there isn't much testosterone around here."

"Well, I'll see what I can do. Now, if you'll direct me to the nearest lumberyard." He paused. "Wait, why don't you go with us and I'll treat you both to lunch?"

She blinked in surprise. "No. I mean this is for you two."

"I don't want to exclude you, Mallory. You're his mother. We need to show Ryan we all get along."

Mallory already knew she could get along with this man. Too well. She recalled their shared kisses just the night before. But any more involvement could be disastrous for all of them. She carried too many scars from her failed marriage. And she doubted he'd ever completely forgive her. But for Ryan's sake she was going to make this time together work.

"Okay, I'd love to go, but I'm paying for half the lumber."

"No way," he argued. "If you do, then you have to help us build it."

"Okay, you win, but I get to test it for sturdiness. If it doesn't meet my standards, it comes down."

He sobered. "That's one thing you don't have to worry about, Mallory. I'd never put our son in harm's way."

She sighed, seeing his heart-wrenching look. "I know you wouldn't, Chase. I guess I'm a little overprotective. It's just been Ryan and me for a long time."

He came to her. "I'm not trying to take him away from you, Mallory I just want to be a part of his life. I want to be his father."

An hour later, Chase, Mallory and Ryan were sitting in a booth at the local diner, eating hamburgers. Chase glanced out the window to see the bed of his truck loaded down with lumber.

"You sure you got enough supplies?" Mallory asked, fighting a smile.

So he'd gone a little overboard. "I think so. We're not sure how big we want it, yet."

"Yeah, Mom," Ryan said. "We're not sure."

Mallory played with the straw in her glass. "I can understand that. Is it going to be a one or two-bedroom? And you'll need to think about property values in the area."

Chase enjoyed her humor, even if it was at his expense. "Very funny. But you wanted it sturdy, I'm making sure it's sturdy."

"Just don't make it so nice he'll move out there permanently."

The boy stopped eating. "But I want to sleep out there," he said. "Chase said we could—" his voice faded, as he realized he was giving away the secret.

Chase was surprised that Mallory just smiled. "Seems you got talked into a lot." Her gaze met Chase's and she lowered her voice. "Eventually, you're going to have to say no to him."

He couldn't take his eyes off her mouth. "I know, but I'm just having too much fun."

They both looked at Ryan as he attacked his hamburger. "That's it, son. Eat up," Chase said. "You're going to need your strength when you swing that hammer."

"I know." The boy chewed another bite. "Can we start on the tree house when we get back?"

"We'll see, but there's rain predicted."

"If it doesn't rain, can we?"

So many questions. "We can start." Across the diner, Chase caught an older woman watching them. She looked to be in her sixties. She had dark hair streaked with gray and a stocky build. There was a frown on her lined face as her eyes riveted on Ryan.

"Oh, no, not now," Mallory whispered under her breath. "It's time to leave." She nudged at Chase.

When the woman started to walk toward them, Chase pulled his wallet from his pocket, took out a twenty-dollar bill, and put it with the check. "Ryan, why don't you go pay for lunch so we can get started back?"

Nodding, the boy slid out of the booth, grabbed the money and took off. The woman looked curiously at

Ryan, but continued to their table. "Well, so you have the gall to show your face in town."

Mallory sighed. "Becky, I have as much right to be here as you do."

The older woman's eyes narrowed. "My son had rights, too, but you took them away."

Mallory's body stiffened, but Chase saw her hands tremble as she clutched them in her lap. "Alan took a lot from me, too." She released a tired breath. "Can't we just let him rest in peace?"

"There's no peace," she said angrily. "I lost my son, but you still have yours. You even managed to take the child away from us."

"I didn't take anyone away," Mallory said in a quiet voice.

Becky turned her glare on Chase. He had no doubt the woman had figured out his part in all this. "I'd say you're the boy's real father."

He just remained silent…for now.

"Too bad you didn't show up sooner, then my son wouldn't have suffered with this woman." Before he could react, she turned and marched off.

Chase wasn't sure what to do. He shot a quick look at Mallory who was blinking away the threatening tears.

"I guess you need to get in line. Seems I messed up a lot of lives with my choices."

Before Chase had a chance to react, she slid out the other side of the booth and hurried to Ryan at the cash register.

Whether she deserved it or not, he didn't like seeing

her hurting. One thing he knew for sure, Mallory was the one who'd suffered the most from those choices.

That afternoon, Mallory sat in her office. The room had once been the study, but the space was big enough for both Liz and herself. She especially liked the location of her desk, right in front of the big window that overlooked the ranch. She could see Liz working in the arena, and off beside the barn, she found Chase and Ryan, digging holes for the posts.

It was hard to concentrate on her upcoming schedule since the man had stripped off his shirt, revealing a muscular chest and arms. His broad back wasn't bad, either. Of course, she knew he had to keep in shape for his job. She just didn't expect it to affect her so much.

Turning her attention to her son, Mallory noticed that he'd removed his shirt, too. Normally, she'd worry about sunscreen, but they were working in the shade of the tree.

Mallory stood and walked away from the window. "Stop it. Just let them do their thing. They don't need you to interfere in their fun."

If only she didn't feel like she was losing a part of Ryan. Was she jealous because the man she once loved and wanted to marry only wanted their son?

If she were honest, she'd admit how much she wanted them to be a family. Okay, maybe not in the traditional sense. She didn't know if she could ever trust herself with a man again. Even Chase.

Especially after the near disaster in the diner. She'd always known Becky Hagan had it in for her. Although Buck and Al Hagan had been friends and business associates, Alan's mother had been against the marriage. No one was good enough for her precious son. Things got worse after the separation.

The slam of the screen door alerted Mallory to Ryan's arrival. She closed her laptop and walked out into the hall, then through the dining room with the dark stained wainscoting and woodwork. There was a huge table that seated ten easily, along with a matching sideboard that had been in Liz's family for generations.

She heard laughter as she stepped into the kitchen, finding Chase and Ryan making sandwiches, peanut butter and jelly. The simple sight make her chest tighten. They smiled alike, with the same brown eyes.

Ryan looked up. "Oh, hi, Mom. Chase and me got hungry." He placed a slice of bread on top of his creation and took a big bite.

"Hope you don't mind," Chase said.

Her pulse raced and she couldn't slow it. "Of course not." She went to the refrigerator and pulled out some milk. "You've been working for hours." She got two glasses from the cupboard and filled them, then took their drinks to their place at the counter. "Get much done?"

"We dug the post holes and set them in cement," Chase said. "The cement needs to dry, then tomorrow, we can frame the base."

He bit into the bread and chewed. How could a man look so sexy eating peanut butter and jelly? Her gaze roamed over him. He leaned against the counter in low-riding jeans with his shirt unbuttoned, exposing just a hint of his muscular chest and rippled stomach.

"Mallory…"

She quickly redirected her attention to his face. "Did you say something?"

He tossed her one of those rare smiles. "I just asked about your afternoon."

"Oh, I stayed busy. I've got a client coming by in a few days to look at one of Liz's colts."

"Oh, no, not Sets Off Sparks," Ryan gasped.

Mallory nodded. "Mr. Paterson wants a good mount for Western Dressage."

Ryan hung his head. "I wanted to keep him."

"And I told you earlier we need to make money to keep the ranch going, or keep your stomach full."

She poked teasingly at her eight-year-old. "But I wouldn't be surprised if the new owner hires Liz to help with the training. So the colt will be around for a while."

"Good."

"And I think…" She wrinkled her nose at Ryan. "That you should take a bath before supper."

"Aw, Mom. Do I have to?"

She sniffed again. "Oh, yes, you have to."

"You know, that's not a bad idea," Chase began. "I'm pretty ripe myself. A shower would cool me off, too. And I may just rest for a little while."

Chase watched as Ryan reluctantly agreed, then finished off his milk, and headed up the stairs for the dreaded bath.

Mallory turned to him and those green eyes locked with his. "Thanks for the help," she said. "He's been going nonstop since the roundup. So have you. You've got to be tired, too."

"It's a good kind of tired," he said, recalling how he'd

been too restless last night after their shared kisses to get much sleep. Suddenly his body stirred at the memory at her tempting mouth…her body. "I wouldn't mind some quiet time." What he wanted was to share more time with Mallory.

Although she didn't seem to feel the same. She moved around the kitchen, cleaning up the mess, and avoiding him. Everything had been going fine between them until they'd gone to lunch. Until her past reared its ugly head.

"Tomorrow afternoon Ryan goes in to the therapist."

Chase knew it was a good idea to talk about the kidnapping. "Has he been having any more nightmares?"

She shook her head. "At least something is going good."

He knew she wasn't talking about Ryan. He carried his plate and glass to the sink where she was staying busy. "Mallory, I'm sorry about what happened at the diner."

She glanced at him, then finally shrugged. "You have nothing to be sorry about. It's my problem."

"Still, no one has a right to talk to you like that." He inhaled her soft scent and he had trouble concentrating. "So…I take it Becky was your mother-in-law."

She nodded and continued to wash. "Although my dad and Alan's dad were business partners at one time, Becky Hagan had never been happy about my marrying her precious son. She blames me for Alan's car accident."

"Were you driving the vehicle?"

"No. But he started drinking heavily after he learned he couldn't father a child."

"Once again, you didn't force your ex to drink, or to get into the car."

She set a washed glass on the counter and shut her

eyes. "I should have stopped him, but he was so angry—" She paused and took a breath. "We'd already separated and Ryan and I were living here, but he kept coming by…at all hours."

Chase tensed. How bad had the man terrorized her? He hated to think that Hagan had his hands on her. Damn, no one deserved to go through that. "Did he hurt you?"

She finally turned to him. "I got out, Chase. I got Ryan out." Her gaze was intense. "You have to know, I would never let anything happen to him."

This was killing him. "I know, darlin'." No matter what happened to her, she'd never let anything happen to their son. "But what about you, Mallory? Did you truly get out?"

She shook her head and started to leave, but he reached out to touch her arm.

"It's okay, you don't have to tell me. Just know that you aren't to blame for what happened."

He couldn't stop himself as he reached out and cupped her jaw. She was so soft. Bravely she bit down on her trembling lip.

He was losing it. The last thing he needed right now was to start up anything with her that didn't pertain to their child. What she needed in a man, he couldn't give her, but that didn't stop his desire for her. Some things hadn't changed.

With the last of his common sense, he dropped his hand. "I should go." But before he could get his feet moving, his cell phone rang. He pulled it off his belt, and saw that it was from the office.

"I need to take this." He walked to the back door.

"Landon," he said.

"Chase, it's Jesse."

"What's up?" He knew it had to be important for his partner to call him on vacation.

"Just a heads-up. I'm going to Sweetwater Friday to see Reyes." There was a long pause. "He'd rather talk with you."

Chase wasn't going to get excited. "Then he better come up with something worth hearing. I'll only give him what he wants, if he gives me something. At least a name, some kind of proof that he knows who shot Wade."

"I'll let you know if that happens. Later." Jesse ended the call.

Chase slipped his phone back in its holder and looked over his shoulder at Mallory. "Sorry."

"Why be sorry? You have a job, too."

Surprisingly, it was a job he hadn't been thinking about much. Not since he came here. He thought about the fun he had spending the day with Ryan. "Yeah. For a long time it was all I had."

"Is there a problem? Is that why they called you?"

He shrugged. "One of the prisoners who took Ryan says he knew my uncle. He wants to talk to me."

Her cat-green eyes widened. "Will you have to go back?"

"Trying to get rid of me?"

For a long time she just stared at him. "No. It's nice having you here…for Ryan."

He walked back to her. "Just for Ryan, Mallory?" He was crazy for doing this, but he couldn't seem to stop himself. "What do you feel about me being here?"

"I told you, Chase, you're welcome here any time," she hedged. "But that's all I can give you."

Two days later, Mallory was up with the sun. So was the father-and-son construction team. They were busy at work beside the barn. It was hard, but she tried not to be too nosey about the project. The platform had gone up yesterday. This morning they'd been working on the stairs.

She also tried to stay away for another reason. To protect herself. She wasn't ready to share any more of her past with Chase. She knew a lot of the problems in her marriage hadn't been her fault, but the emotional scars would take a long time to heal…if ever.

"Is this the best price?"

She shook away her thoughts, and turned back to Jerry Patterson, the buyer for Sets Off Sparks. "Not only is the price set, it's a great price for a horse with his bloodline." Jerry always had to feel he was getting a deal, especially if he was doing business with a woman. But eventually Mallory could bring him around to her way of thinking. And he could afford the colt at any price. "And…Liz is giving you a deal on the training. I'd say take it, because if you don't, she's had two other offers."

The forty-something, local rancher grinned. "You're good, Mallory. I hope Liz knows what a great salesperson you are."

"What Liz knows is top quality stock. I just sell them."

"Well, you can stamp *sold* on this animal." He pointed over his shoulder. "Hopefully he'll turn into an AQHA reigning champion."

"I don't doubt it." She started walking Jerry back to his truck. He usually wanted to hang around and chat. She didn't have the time, especially since he'd been trying to get her to go out on a date for the past six months. About the time his second divorce became final.

Jerry glanced toward the barn. "Looks like your boy is getting a mighty fine tree house. Is one of the hands helping him?"

The fact he thought Chase was a hand bothered her. "Ryan's helper isn't a ranch hand. Chase Landon is a Texas Ranger." That was all she was going to say.

The tall rancher stared down at her, then finally said, "I guess that about says it all. The ranger is a lucky man."

It wasn't a big deal Jerry thought she was dating Chase, she told herself. "It's still a new relationship."

"Well, he must be special if he got your attention. I wish the best for both of you."

She nodded. "Thanks, Jerry." Behind him she saw Ryan and Chase coming toward them. Oh, no.

"Hey, Mom. Chase needs to go back to the lumber-yard. Can I go?"

"Sure."

"Hi, Mr. Patterson."

"Hello, son," Jerry said, tugging on Ryan's hat. "Looks like you're getting quite the tree house."

Mallory knew Ryan had never cared for Jerry's teasing. "Yeah, it is."

She jumped in. "Ryan, go wash up, then you can leave." She nudged her son toward the house, but then saw Chase was approaching them. The day was just getting worse. He put on his shirt and was buttoning it.

Jerry smiled. "Looks like I get to meet the guy who finally caught Mallory's attention." He held out his hand. "Jerry Patterson."

"Chase Landon." He shook the offered hand.

"You're a lucky man to win a gal like Mallory."

Mallory's heart pounded as Chase's gaze caught hers. "Yes, I am lucky." He took two steps and stood beside her, then slipped his arm around her. "And Ryan's a bonus, too." He looked down at her upturned face.

Was he going to go along with her fib? "I was just telling Jerry that you came to visit." She shrugged. "He just sort of guessed something was going on." She laughed nervously.

"It's kind of hard to hide my feelings." He placed a quick kiss on her mouth. "Right, darlin'?"

"Well, I can see I'm not wanted here." Jerry tipped his hat then walked to his truck. Smiling, they both kept watching as the man climbed into the truck.

"You can let go," Mallory insisted, glued to Chase's side.

"Not yet," he told her. "We need to prove to him that you're taken." He turned her in his arms and his mouth closed over hers.

CHAPTER SEVEN

MALLORY'S HEART RACED as Chase's mouth captured hers in a hungry kiss. In an instant, she was lost in his arms, and wanting more. He didn't disappoint her. When he ran his tongue over the seam of her lips, her hands found their way around his neck and she held on for the wild ride. She loved his familiar taste, the feelings he invoked in her. Inhaling his masculine scent of soap, sweat and pure Chase, she felt alive.

Finally he broke off the kiss, but stayed close and whispered, "You think we convinced him?"

"What?" Mallory opened her eyes to see his smoldering dark eyes. "Oh—" She stepped back. "You shouldn't have done that."

He raised an eyebrow. "The kiss? I thought you wanted Jerry to think you had a boyfriend. Didn't you?"

"Yes, I did, but you didn't need to…kiss me," she stumbled over her words. "I was handling things just fine before you got here."

He folded his arms over his chest. "Maybe so, but now he knows you're taken." He leaned closer. "No need to thank me, it was my pleasure."

Before she could speak, Ryan came racing out of the house. "I'm ready to go."

"Good." He looked back at Mallory as Ryan ran off toward the truck. "Would you like to go with us? Maybe I can warn off any other guys who are interested in you."

She was fuming. "Thank you, but I can handle things from now on. I need to catch up on some work, so I'll stay here. I'm working on a list of horses for you to check out."

"Good. I'm looking forward to it. See you later." He hurried off to catch up with Ryan.

"Bye, Mom." Her son waved.

She watched the two of them and her heart soared. The sad fact was as much as she wanted both of them, she could only have one. And soon, she'd have to share her son's attention with his father.

Liz came up beside her. "So did Jerry decide on the colt?"

"Yeah. But you know Jerry, he doesn't make the sale easy."

"That's because he's sizing you up to be wife number three."

"I quickly nixed that idea."

"I know, I saw Chase." Liz tipped her hat back. "Nothing like a big, handsome Texas Ranger to ward off any unwanted suitors."

Oh, no. "I really didn't plan for Chase to get involved. I just led Jerry in that direction, then Chase showed up and took it another step."

"No kidding." She grinned. "That was quite a kiss."

Mallory was embarrassed. "It wasn't what it looked like."

"It looked like a kiss." She released a sigh. "Like a mouthwatering, heart-stopping, one that leads-to-other-things, kiss." She turned to Mallory. "Just admit you enjoyed it."

Mallory couldn't deny it. "Yes, I did." She sobered. "But it still isn't wise. Chase doesn't feel—"

"There you go again, overanalyzing everything. Believe me, Mallory, from what I saw, Chase Landon didn't act like that kiss was such a chore."

"He's still angry with me about Ryan."

They started walking toward the house. "He probably is. But I also see how he looks at you, and I think that anger is his protection against his feelings. I'd say go after that man, he's a keeper."

Mallory didn't want to think about starting up a relationship with Chase. He'd hurt her so badly before she couldn't stand it again. "I went after him once before, and look how that turned out."

Liz paused on the porch steps. "Yeah, you two got a great kid."

"Do you think Mom will like it?" Ryan asked as he paused from hammering a nail in the railing. His baseball cap was turned backward on his head, exposing a face smudged with dirt, and tiny beads of sweat across his nose.

"What's not to like?"

He grinned. "It's so cool."

Ryan raised his hand and they exchanged a high five.

"Yeah, cool." Chase glanced over the solid tongue-and-groove pine flooring. The two-by-four railing was

up all around the sides. The structure had been rein-
forced so many times, he'd lost count. But he wanted it
safe for the boy, especially when he wasn't around to
protect him.

"Chase, when can the walls go up?"

"Not today. It's getting too hot to work much later."

Ryan looked disappointed. "What about tomorrow?
Can we work on it then?"

Chase had been at the ranch for five days, and he'd
counted himself lucky to spend most of that time with
his son. "Sure. We'll get it finished before I leave."

The boy looked away, but not before he saw the
sadness in his eyes.

"What's the matter?" Chase asked.

Ryan shrugged. "I wish you didn't have to go back
to Midland. I like it that you're here all the time."

Chase liked that, too. "I have to go back, Ryan. I have
a job. Just like you have to go back to school."

He sighed. "I know…."

Chase took off his hat and wiped his forehead on his
sleeve. He sat down on the edge of the platform, then
patted the spot next to him. Ryan took the offered seat.
"We've talked about this, son." The endearment he
called Ryan took on new meaning these days. "I'm only
here for a visit. But I'll see you again when you come
to your grandfather's ranch."

"I know…it's just that all my friends…Bobbie, Jason
and Curt, they all got their dads around. I mean this is
the first time I ever got to build something like this." The
boy tilted his head up to Chase, his throat worked hard
as he swallowed. "'Cause I don't have a dad."

Chase fought his own emotions. "I'm sorry, Ryan. I know what that's like. My dad wasn't around, either."

There was a long pause, then Ryan said, "You didn't have anyone, either?"

"I had my uncle."

The boy looked thoughtful. "I guess I have my grandpa, too."

They sat there for a few minutes, then Ryan said, "I saw you kiss Mom…and I thought if you really like her maybe you'd come back a lot. I mean she's really pretty…."

It was crazy, but Chase felt embarrassed. Not that he thought it was wrong to kiss Mallory. He just didn't know how to explain his feelings to the boy. Not when he didn't know himself.

The child went on to explain, "Mr. Patterson likes Mom, too, but I don't like him." He shook his head. "I'm glad you kissed her."

Chase couldn't help but smile. "I'm glad I kissed her, too."

Ryan's eyes rounded. "So are you going to be her boyfriend?"

Chase didn't want to deal with that question. He was still too mixed up about his anger. How could they start something, and keep it going when they lived so far apart? He tugged at Ryan's baseball cap. "You ask too many questions."

"I know, but I like talking to you. You know how guys talk." The boy looked down again and poked his finger at one of the knots in the wood. "You know what else— I wish? That you were my dad."

"Ryan…" Chase's chest tightened, his throat dried

up. He'd never experienced this feeling before. He wanted so badly to tell him the truth.

The boy still didn't look at him. "I don't remember my dad too much. I remember my mom used to cry a lot."

"You remember that?"

Ryan jerked his head in a nod. "I mean, I was just a little kid, but I sort of remember she got scared. But then we came to live with Aunt Liz and everything was better. Except one time Mom had to talk to the sheriff…she didn't let Dad come here." His gaze met Chase's. "You wouldn't do that, because I know you'd be nice to her…and me."

"Do you miss him?" Chase couldn't manage to say the word, *father*.

"No." His innocent gaze raised to Chase. "Is that bad?"

"No, it's not bad." He put his arm around Ryan's shoulders and hugged him close. "A father should be there for his kid." Chase was feeling his own guilt.

"I know. Mom says she's sorry he wasn't a better dad for me." The boy sniffed. "I used to be sad because he didn't want me…. Was it my fault that he didn't like me?"

"Oh, Ryan, don't ever think that. You're a great kid. Anyone would be proud of you."

"Really?"

Chase had to nod because he couldn't get the words out. If there was any doubt before, there wasn't any now. He loved this child.

"Hey, you two," a familiar voice called. "How come you aren't working?"

Chase looked down to see Mallory standing under the tree below.

Ryan stood up. "Hey, Mom. Look, the floor is done. But it's too hot to work anymore today."

"I don't blame you," she said. She glanced around at the structure, then turned to Chase. "It looks good."

Chase's emotions were still pretty raw, and a lot of it was directed at Mallory. "Does it meet your approval?"

"Yes, and it's even better. Can't wait to see it finished."

"A few more days."

"Well, since you're finished for today, how about a swim?"

"Sure, but where?" Ryan asked.

"Bobbie's mom called and invited us over for swimming and a barbecue." She paused. "All of us."

Ryan looked at Chase. "Wow. It's like we're a real family."

Later that afternoon, Mallory sat at the edge of the shallow end of the Everetts' pool. She was wearing a modest aqua-colored, one-piece suit, but she wasn't keen on swimming with a half-dozen splashing kids. She'd leave that to Chase and Bobbie's father, Robert.

"They should be exhausted by supper," Meg Everett said as she sat down beside Mallory and dangled her feet in the water.

She was a pretty blonde with a warm smile and a friendly manner. She'd married her high school sweetheart and had two great kids, and was probably Mallory's closest friend, outside of Liz.

"Oh, I don't know. Ryan's been going like this since school let out."

For a long time they both watched the antics in the pool between the fathers and sons.

Meg spoke first. "I've never seen a Texas Ranger without his hat and badge. I'm impressed."

It was hard not to be. Chase had wide shoulders and a muscular chest and that flat washboard stomach. A strange feeling stirred in her stomach. "They have to stay in shape," she answered honestly.

"He seems to care about Ryan. They're like father and son." Meg turned to Mallory. "It's really great, isn't it?"

Meg wasn't stupid. She could see the obvious, that the two were related. "So far, but it may not be down the road."

Her friend smiled. "If I were you I wouldn't let the man get very far away. It's easy to see he cares about Ryan…and you."

Mallory couldn't think about a relationship with Chase. It was her son who needed a father. She didn't need a man.

Suddenly a stream of cold water startled them. She looked out in the pool to catch Ryan and Chase smiling at her.

"Why not come in the water?" Chase asked.

"I'm fine right here."

Robert and Bobbie appeared. "Come on, Mom," Bobbie said, waving for Meg.

"I'm being summoned," her friend said and waded in as she pulled her hair up into a ponytail.

Envious, Mallory watched the other couple at play. It seemed she wasn't going to be left out as Chase came up to her. He stood in the shallow end, looking all tan and gorgeous. There was a swirl of dark hair on his perfectly sculpted chest. She had trouble breathing.

"If you won't come into the water, I guess I'll have to bring you." She gasped as he scooped her up in his arms. She could hear Ryan's cheers and laughter as Chase carried her to the deep end.

She ignored the cool water because Chase held her close. Too close. She could hear Ryan's cheers.

"You think just because you're stronger than me, you can manhandle me."

"I've never manhandled a woman in my life," he told her, then leaned in and whispered against her ear. "This is called gentle persuasion. Damn, but you feel good."

She pulled back and looked at him as the water rose to their necks. "Maybe you should put me down."

"No, you feel fine just where you are."

"Mom… Mom…"

She jerked around to see Ryan and the other kids wrapped in their towels at the side of the pool. "We're gonna go inside to play video games. You stay here with Chase and swim, okay?"

She managed a nod, then looked back at Chase. "Maybe I should get out, too."

"You should stay here," he told her. "Our son can entertain himself for a while." He let go of her legs and turned her to face him. "Wrap your legs around my waist."

"Chase…this isn't a good idea." She glanced at Robert and Meg. They were at the other end of the pool, cuddled together talking softly.

"Relax…just enjoy it." His hand circled her legs and

guided them around him. "We aren't doing anything wrong…yet."

Up close, she eyed him sternly. How could she relax with her body tucked against his? She found herself swaying forward as he pressed his hand in the small of her back, nudging her closer. Their eyes locked for a long time, his dark and smoky. Her fingers moved around his neck and locked together as his mouth dipped and pressed a kiss against her mouth. It was only a whisper of a touch before he pulled back.

"Hold on," he told her, then he caught her by surprise. He pushed off backward, causing her to end up on top of him. With a gasp, she managed to tighten her grip around his neck. A warm shiver surged through her as her body made contact with every inch of him…intimately.

His gaze locked with hers, telling her he felt it, too. "It's still there, Mallory. Whether we like or not, there's something between us."

She closed her eyes. At one time she'd have given anything to hear him say those words. "Please, Chase, just let it die. Too much has happened, too much resentment."

He moved them to the side of the pool, gripping the ledge. "How can it be too late, Mal? Not when I lay awake at night, thinking about you, remembering how it was to make love to you."

She sucked in a breath. "Chase, please…"

He didn't stop. His hand moved over her back, keeping their bodies connected. "I can't keep my hands off you. Even our son has noticed what's going on. He saw me kissing you the other day."

She glared at him. "What did he say?"

"He wants me to pursue you. He doesn't like Jerry. I don't either."

"Well, it's not your business." She started to pull away, but he held her tight.

"You made it my business, Mallory. So if Ryan doesn't like him around I don't either."

"So now you're dictating who I date?"

"No, but I can do something to make you forget any other man." His mouth captured hers in a hungry kiss. She wanted to protest, but telling herself that she didn't want to make a scene in the pool, she didn't stop him.

In truth, she wanted Chase to kiss her. And what did that make her? A woman still in love with a man who would never forgive her for not telling him about his son. She didn't blame him. How could she when she couldn't forgive herself.

It was after nine when the Everetts walked Chase and Mallory out to the truck. A giggling Ryan and Bobbie followed close behind.

Chase found he didn't want this evening to end. He'd spent a nearly perfect day with his son…and Mallory. He also knew that he'd taken advantage of her when they'd been in the pool. He didn't know what had come over him.

That was a big lie. Truth was, he'd never been able to resist Mallory Kendall. Nine years later, that hadn't changed. Except there was more at stake now. His son's future happiness.

Mallory turned to Meg. "Are you sure you want to keep Ryan overnight?"

"Yes, we do," the blonde told her. "Bobbie's been wanting this sleepover since Ryan got home." She glanced at Chase. "It seems he's been pretty busy with this secret project of his."

"I'm sure Bobbie will get an invitation when it's finished."

"I think we'd all like to see it," Robert told him.

"You will, right, Ryan?"

The boy came over to Chase. "Right. And I'll be home tomorrow…early. Mr. Everett said he'll take when me he goes to work."

"I won't start without you."

"Okay." Ryan glanced around at the group and motioned to Chase to follow him. Once alone, he said, "It looked like you and Mom had fun today."

So the little stinker had set him up. "Yes, we had a good time."

The boy grinned. "Now, you don't have to worry about me tonight. Maybe…you can take her out…if you want…."

Chase tried to act indifferent. "I think I can handle this part on my own."

"Okay, but if you need to know anything," the boy told him, "I know what Mom likes."

Chase was intrigued. "What does she like?"

He looked thoughtful. "Daisies. Her favorite color is pink. And she likes butterflies, too. A lot. She collects them. Her favorite is a glass one that has all these pretty colors inside. I can't even pick it up. She keeps it on the table next to her bed."

Chase's chest tightened. He remembered all those

vivid colors, too. He'd given her that butterfly for her birthday. So she still had it.

"Ryan," Mallory called to him.

They walked back. "What, Mom?"

"Just wanted to say good-night." She kissed him.

"Good night, Mom, Chase." He went to stand with Bobbie. Ryan's friend had curly blond hair and a stocky build. And according his son, they'd been best friends since kindergarten.

"Thank you for a great day and a wonderful supper," Chase said as he shook Robert's hand.

"You're welcome any time," Robert said.

Chase handed him a business card. "If you're in Midland stop by the office and I'll show you around."

Robert grinned. "You can count on it. Bobbie would love it."

With his hand against the small of Mallory's back, Chase escorted her to the truck and helped her in.

Funny, he'd never gone for much of the couples thing. Girls he'd dated in the past went with him to ranger parties as a group thing. Today was different. The Everetts saw them as a couple. Of course the way he'd kissed Mallory in the pool, he shouldn't doubt it. Door shut, he walked around to the other side and climbed in.

He started the truck, then turned to Mallory. "I think we need to talk about—" He suddenly noticed the soft hair floating around her face. Her eyes were intense with desire.

It hit him like fire in his gut. "You better stop looking at me like that, or we'll never make it home."

CHAPTER EIGHT

THE TRIP BACK to the ranch seemed to take forever, but Mallory was glad. She needed time to think. If she went with Chase to the cottage everything would change between them. She knew he wanted her body, but did he want her? Did he want her for a lifetime?

And was she ready for this?

Chase drove the truck under the archway and her heart pounded so hard she knew he could hear it. She would be foolish to go with him, but knew that wouldn't stop her.

Once in front of the cottage, he shut off the engine and turned toward her. Silence hung in the humid air. She knew what he wanted from her. He didn't say a word as he reached out and pulled her into his arms. When his mouth came down on hers, she knew she wasn't going to deny him…ever.

When he finally released her, she was almost dizzy. He climbed out of the truck and pulled her after him. On the ground, he wrapped his arm around her and led her up to the porch, then through the unlocked door. Inside, he closed out the world with the click of the door latch. In the darkness, he reached for her, then covered her mouth in another hungry kiss.

Her heartbeat quickened as her arms found their way up his chest and around his neck as he nibbled on her lips. She whimpered and returned his fervor. No doubt, she wanted him, she'd always wanted Chase. As his tongue slipped into her mouth, his skilled hands moved over her body, causing unbelievable sensations.

He broke off the kiss. "I want you, Mallory," he breathed.

She searched for the last of her common sense. "This isn't wise, Chase. We have so much to work out…."

He moved against her, letting her feel his desire. "Right now this is all I want to think about, just you and me." He kissed her tenderly, then raised his head. With only the moonlight, she saw his silhouette, felt his breath against her cheek. "This is a start, Mallory."

"What if… Oh, God—"

Her words died off as his hand moved under her T-shirt to her breast, stroking her through the lace. Her nipple hardened immediately and she pushed against his hand, aching for more.

He cupped her breast, then leaned down and drew the nipple into his mouth, sucking gently. She moaned and gripped his arms to keep from crumbling to the floor.

"Just tell me you want me to stop," he said. "And I'll walk you back to the house." He groaned and rested his head against hers. "Please…don't, Mal. I'll die… right here."

"So would I," she admitted.

He tugged the material over her head, then released the clasp on her bra and let it drop to the floor.

Her hands went to his shirt and pulled it from his jeans. "I'll need to help you catch up, so I can drive you crazy."

She could feel his grin. "Then let me help you, ma'am." He jerked the long shirttails from his pants, and she pushed the material off his wide shoulders.

She drew in a sharp breath. He was beautiful. Her hands went to his chest, feeling his solid heat, the rapid beating of his heart.

Chase sucked air into his lungs, trying to hold it together as her hands moved slowly over his skin. Mallory was like a fever in his blood. She'd always had that effect on him. But there was so much more at stake now. She'd been hurt badly, and they had a son to think about. He knew he had to earn her trust again.

She placed her lips on his flat nipple and sucked gently. That was it. He couldn't take it any more. He raised her head to greet her with a searing kiss. His hunger for her was well past the point of playfulness.

Once he released her, he lifted her in his arms, carried her into the bedroom and lay her down on the mattress. He flicked on the table lamp, filling the room with a soft glow, silhouetting her in the bed.

He searched her lovely body, and stopped at her face. "Never doubt that I never stopped wanting you, Mallory."

She blinked. "I never stopped wanting you, either. Oh, Chase, I wish—"

He stretched out beside her. "No regrets. No past. I think tonight it is just for us…the here and now."

She nodded and he smiled. But all he was thinking about was more and that he wasn't about to let her go again.

The next morning, the sun wasn't up yet, so Mallory thought she could make a quiet exit. Wrong.

"Trying to sneak out on me?"

She swung around. Chase was sitting up in bed, only a sheet covering the lower half of his magnificent body.

"Chase, I didn't want to wake you. I was just—" She pointed over her shoulder. "I should get back to the house. Ryan will be home soon."

"Our son isn't coming for another few hours." Reclining, he propped his head on his hand and smiled up at her. "You were running away, admit it."

Her face flamed. "Not exactly… Maybe this wasn't such a good idea."

"You mean us spending the night together making incredible love?" He sighed. "Oh, yeah, that was such a rotten idea."

Mallory couldn't help smiling. So did he. "I just thought it would be better." She sobered. "Everything is so complicated…with Ryan and…you."

He stared at her for a moment, then motioned for her to come to him. Foolishly, she did. He grabbed her hand and pulled her onto the bed. Before she realized what was happening, he pinned her body with his.

"What's the matter, Mallory, did I get to you?"

Yes! Yes! And yes! "Get over yourself, Landon." She tried to get free, but it was useless. "I have work to do."

"You couldn't even kiss me goodbye?"

"You were asleep." And he'd looked far too tempting.

"I'm wide awake now. So can I talk you into breakfast in bed?"

Pressed up against him, she felt the evidence of his idea of breakfast. She couldn't let this happen…again. She was in too deep as it was and needed to get away to find some perspective. To think.

"I think it's safer if we have breakfast at the house with Liz. So, please, let me go."

"Then at least give me a good-morning kiss."

She closed her eyes. "Chase, this isn't a good idea. Ryan is expected home soon."

"Our son would be tickled to see us getting along."

That was what she was afraid of. Ryan getting hurt when the two weeks ended and Chase went back to Midland. "And what about when you leave?"

Chase's sexy bedroom eyes locked with hers and she felt her insides quake. He leaned down and brushed his mouth against hers. "Who knows, maybe we can work something out…. Don't you want to see where this will lead?" Before she could say anything, he leaned down and this time captured her mouth in a mind-blowing kiss that had her aching for him and believing they could work this out. But she'd already given everything up for a man. She couldn't lose herself again. No matter how much she loved him.

With the last of her strength, she pulled away. "Stop, Chase. Please. I can't do this."

He let go of her and she climbed off the bed. She brushed her hair back. "I'm sorry. Everything is happening so fast. And what we really need to think about is Ryan." She paused, not knowing what else to say. She loved this man. And that was what had her frightened more than anything else. "I've got to go." She turned and rushed out, not stopping until she got to her bedroom at the house.

Closing the door, she collapsed on the bed. She had done it now. A tear fell. She had fallen in love with Chase again. And the pain would only be worse when he left her for the second time.

Two mornings later, Chase stood back to examine his work. It was finally looking like a tree house. The door and windows needed to be framed, along with a coat of sealer to protect the wood. But it was close enough to finished to satisfy Ryan.

"What did you do to my mom?"

Chase turned around to find an angry-looking Ryan.

"Why? What's wrong with your mother?" he asked. He hadn't seen her since the morning after they'd made love.

"She's sad again. And she won't tell me what's wrong. I thought you liked her."

This was crazy. He wasn't used to explaining himself to an eight-year-old. "I do," he admitted honestly. "But it's more complicated sthan just that."

The boy placed his hand on his hips. "I hate it when grown-ups say that. Why don't you just kiss her again and tell her how much you like her?"

"I've already done that," Chase said a little too angry. He lowered his voice. "I don't think your mom wants a man in her life right now. Outside of you, of course."

The child's expression turned sad. "But I want you

to come back here and see me. I want—" Tears flooded his eyes and he turned and started to leave. Chase grabbed him.

"Leave me alone," Ryan cried, fighting him.

Chase's heart was breaking. "I'm not going to leave you, Ryan. I'm never going to leave you, son."

Finally the boy wrapped his arms around Chase's waist and buried his face against his stomach. "Yes, you will. It will be just me and Mom. I thought you were different…. I wanted you to be my dad."

Emotions welled inside of Chase as he hugged him close. This was killing him, and it couldn't go on. "Ryan, we need to find your mother and talk about this. Is she home?"

Ryan wiped his tears away and stood back. "No, she went to Lubbock. She won't be back until late. Don't say anything to her…she'll just get sad again. Just forget I said anything…."

"No, I won't, Ryan. I care about you."

"Don't say you have to leave. I know that." Fresh tears spilled over. "I should have never started to like you because I knew this would happen…. I don't want a stupid tree house. I don't want you, either. I wish you never came here," he yelled then ran off.

"Ryan—" Chase went after him. He had to tell him the truth. "Ryan."

The boy shot off in the direction of the old pile of wood. He stumbled, but caught his balance, then suddenly he froze with a startled look on his face.

Leery, Chase slowed down and searched the area to

find the reason. His own heart pounded with fear when he saw the coiled rattlesnake about four feet from his son.

"Ryan, just stand there," he said in a soft calming voice. "Don't move, son."

"I'm scared…."

So was he. "I know, son. But believe me, I'm not going to let anything happen to you."

"Hurry."

Chase assessed the situation, and it didn't look good. He didn't have a gun, just a small knife on his belt. What he needed was to draw the snake's attention away from the kid. That could backfire, too. The sound of the rattle let him know the snake wasn't leaving.

He had one chance. Slowly, he came up behind the boy, talking calmly. "Ryan, I'm going to grab you, so don't fight me."

"Okay," the boy answered.

Chase couldn't even breathe, praying he was doing the right thing. He was about a foot from the child as he whipped his arm around Ryan's small frame, and pulled him up and away. He almost made it until he felt the sharp pain in the back of his thigh. Safely away, the snake was gone, but Chase fell to the ground.

"Man, that was cool," Ryan said. But his happiness died when he saw Chase. "What happened?"

"I don't think I'm as quick as I used to be. The rattler got me on the leg. You think you can find Liz? I should go to the hospital."

An hour later, Mallory rushed into the emergency room. Her heart was beating like crazy. It had been since she'd gotten Liz's voice mail that she'd brought in Chase because of a snakebite.

She glanced around to find Ryan and Liz seated in the waiting area and rushed over to them.

"Mom, you're here." Ryan ran to her. "Chase saved me from a snake, but it bit him. So Liz brought him here."

She hugged him tighter. "But you're okay?"

He nodded. "Yes, but it's my fault that Chase got bit. I was running away and he came after me."

She glanced at Liz. "How is Chase doing?"

"He seemed okay when I brought him in. I had the snakebite kit in the tack room." She sighed. "I guess we need to clear the area better so this won't happen again."

Mallory stood. "We live in Texas on a ranch. Snakes come with the territory." She looked at her son. "You have to be more careful."

"I promise. Just don't be mad at Chase. Okay?"

"I'm not mad, but the man seems to be rescuing you a lot." And Mallory owed Chase once again.

"Mom, will you go and see if he's all right?"

"Okay, but I'm not sure they'll tell me how he is." She walked up to the desk. "I was wondering how Chase Landon is doing."

The receptionist barely looked at her. "Are you family?"

She hesitated. "Yes…ah, I'm his wife."

The woman nodded. "I'll let you talk to the doctor." She led her down a hall into a cubicle with the curtain drawn. She stepped behind it and found Chase lying on his side, with his long leg exposed, a bandage on his thigh.

He tried to sit up. "Mallory…"

"Hi." She suddenly felt shy. "Ryan was so worried, he sent me back here. Are you okay?"

"It hurts like the devil, but the doctor says I'll live."

She edged closer to the bed. "Ryan also said you saved him from the snake."

He shrugged. "It would have been worse if the boy was bitten. We almost made it, too." He smiled. "I guess I'm getting slow in my old age."

"Oh, yeah, you're so old." She smiled, too. "Thank you, Chase. Thank you for taking such good care of Ryan."

Chase reached for her hand and laced his fingers with hers. She liked the connection to him. "He's my son, too, Mallory. Don't you know I'd do anything for him? I'll admit I never felt so helpless…and so scared…."

"That's how I feel a lot of times."

His dark eyes searched hers. "You don't have to do this alone any more. I'm here, Mal. I'm going to be a part of Ryan's life. And I want to be a part of your life, too."

She swallowed back her overflowing emotions. She wanted that, too, but her past caused a lot of doubts. "I don't know if I can handle that right now. I don't know if I ever will be…" She saw the hurt in his eyes. "I do know that we need to tell Ryan the truth."

He smiled. "I'd like that. I won't let him down, Mallory, or you."

She knew that in her head, but in her heart she was still afraid. Someone was bound to get hurt.

"You sure you're comfortable?" Ryan asked. "I can get you another pillow."

Chase nodded. "No, I'm fine." He glanced up at Mallory from the guest-room bed. Since leaving the hospital that afternoon, both Mallory and Liz insisted he come and stay at the house during his recuperation. And so they could keep an eye on him. He wasn't used to being taken care of.

Ryan ran out of the room.

"His energy is exhausting."

"You do that to him, Chase. I've never seen him take to anyone as quickly as he has to you. It's time he knows the truth."

He swallowed. "You sure?"

She nodded. "I'm sure. He already loves you."

Dressed in his pajamas, the boy walked back into the room carefully carrying a glass of water. He set it beside the bed on the table. "That's just in case you're thirsty in the middle of the night."

"Thanks, Ryan," Chase said and patted the mattress. "Here, why don't you come sit down next to me. Your mother and I want to talk to you."

The boy climbed on the bed, but was careful to stay away from the Chase's injured leg. "I'm sorry I got mad today, and I'm sorry about what happened to you."

"I know, Ryan, but that's not what we want to talk to you about." Feeling the emotions clogging his throat, Chase looked at Mallory for courage. "Remember when I told you that I knew your mom a long time ago?"

Ryan nodded. "Yeah."

"Well, we dated back then…and we fell in love."

The child looked back and forth between them. "Really?"

"And there's something else, too," Mallory joined in. "Alan wasn't your father," she told him, then took a breath. "Chase is…."

Ryan sat there a long time. His expression told her he was trying to take it all in. "I guess that's why he didn't like me so much, huh?"

Mallory's heart sank as tears filled her eyes. "I'm sorry, honey. I wish I could have made it better."

Ryan didn't seem to hear her as his attention was drawn to Chase. "You're really my dad?" he asked, his eyes rounded in hope and questions.

"Yes, I'm really your dad."

"Did you know about me before now? When I was little?"

Mallory could see that Chase didn't look happy having to answer that question. She sat on the other side of the bed. "No, Ryan. Chase didn't know about you. He went off to be a ranger, and I married Alan… because I didn't know how to find Chase."

He nodded and turned back to Chase. "Do you want to be my dad now? I mean do you want a kid?"

"Yes, and yes," he told him. "But I don't want just any kid, I want you, Ryan…Landon."

Ryan grinned. "Wow, I get your name, too."

"I'd like you to have it," Chase said.

"Sure."

"Do I get to call you Dad, too?"

Chase nodded and drew the boy into his arms. "I love you, son."

"I love you, too, Dad," the boy whispered.

Mallory looked on at the two men in her life. At least for them, all seemed right with the world. For now.

CHAPTER NINE

IT WAS AFTER TEN O'CLOCK when Mallory peered into the bedroom to see Ryan asleep. Finally. It had been a busy day and evening, especially for an eight-year-old.

She smiled, thinking about father and son together. They'd spent most of the evening in the guest room, talking. Only after Chase promised they would work on the tree house in the morning, had Mallory managed to get Ryan off to bed.

She walked down the hall toward her own bedroom, but seeing the light on in the guest room, she stopped to see if Chase needed anything.

Tapping on the door, she waited to hear his voice before she walked in. She paused when she saw he was propped up in the bed, shirtless, that glorious chest of his exposed to her. A hundred delicious thoughts came to mind and her pulse immediately shot off.

He smiled at her. "Well, this is a pleasant surprise."

She gripped the doorknob, trying to keep a safe distance from the man. "I just wanted to know if you needed anything before I turned in."

His dark eyes locked on hers. "Could you stay a minute?"

She hesitated, then walked in and closed the door. "Not too long, I have some work I want to finish up tonight."

"You seem to work a lot."

"Not all of us are on vacation."

He sighed. "And that's going to end soon. I'll have to go back to Midland. I don't want to leave Ryan…." His gaze searched hers. "Or you."

She wasn't ready to discuss anything between them. "Maybe you should just concentrate on Ryan."

"Is that what you want me do? Just forget the other night…us being together?"

She knew this would happen. "We aren't the main focus here, Chase. Ryan is. I don't want our son to get the wrong impression. We can't give him false hope that his parents might get together."

"Come here, Mal." He patted the spot beside him on the bed.

She shook her head. "Why? So you can prove that you can complicate things even more?" she said bravely. "I don't think so."

Chase knew he should leave her alone, but the hell with it, he couldn't. He jerked the sheet away and started to climb out of bed.

"Stop." She rushed to his side and pushed him back against the pillow. "You need to stay in bed."

With her leaning over him, he reached out and touched her cheek. He was encouraged when she didn't pull away. "God. You're beautiful."

She sucked in a breath. "Chase, we can't—"

Chase played dirty. Even knowing Mallory could complicate everything, he still wanted her. "Believe me, I'm controlling myself. If you knew what I really want to do with you…"

Those beautiful green eyes widened. "We can't let anything happen."

"We already have, Mallory. And we both enjoyed it very…very much." He leaned forward and brushed a kiss against her tempting mouth.

She sucked in a breath. "Chase…"

"I love it when you whisper my name…." He craved her like no other woman. Tempted, he nibbled her lips, then when her breathing grew rapid, he deepened the kiss and drew her closer. She tumbled into his arms, and he reveled in her softness against his chest. He feasted on her mouth, tasting her sweetness…her own hunger. Finally he pulled away and looked into those mesmerizing eyes.

"I've never wanted anyone as much as I want you. And if you want me to keep my hands off you, you better leave now."

"It would be the wise thing to do." Her hands moved to his chest, drawing an imaginary pattern with her fingers. "I mean, this can't lead to anything good."

"Oh, I disagree. The way we feel right now is a very good thing. Makes me happy." He placed a kiss on her nose. "And I'm planning on making you happy, too. Very happy."

"What about Ryan?"

"Sssh," he breathed. "Ryan has nothing to do with this. This is you and me, Mallory."

She glanced down at his leg. "What about your injury?"

He pulled her closer. "I'm a Texas Ranger, I'm tough. I can handle it." He grinned. "And you, too." He closed his mouth over hers and proceeded to show her.

The next morning, Chase woke with a jerk and sat up in bed. The sun was already up. He rubbed his hand over his face. His thoughts turned to Mallory and their night together. He glanced to the other side of the bed. Of course it was empty. She'd left him hours ago.

He remembered the soft kiss, then she'd slipped from his arms. He'd hated letting her go. It felt so right, her being there, curled up next to him. His body stirred in memory of their lovemaking. But it wasn't the physical response that bothered him, it was what he felt in the middle of his chest.

Mallory had gotten into his heart…again.

Thing was, had he gotten to her? Did she feel the same about him? Was she willing to work on a relationship with him? There were so many things they needed to talk about, and soon.

He grabbed the pair of neglected pajama bottoms off the floor. He slipped them on and stood. His thigh felt better today. Walking around the room, he found most of the soreness was gone, too.

And in a few days, he would be, too. He only had a little vacation time left. And a promised tree house to finish for Ryan. But first, a shower and some coffee. Before he could gather clean clothes and head for the bathroom, there was a knock on the door.

"Come in," he called.

It wasn't Mallory as he expected, but Jesse Raines. He was juggling two mugs. "Hey, Chase. Sleeping in, I see."

"Hey, Jesse." He went to him and took one of the mugs. "What brings you here?"

"I heard you tangled with a snake."

"Yeah, but he didn't get as much as he wanted." He shook his friend's hand. "Please, don't tell me Robertson sent you here to bring me back."

"No, the captain isn't asking for you. I just thought you'd want to hear what's been going on with Reyes."

Chase motioned for Jesse to sit in the chair. His partner wouldn't make the trip if it wasn't important.

"So what did Reyes have to say?"

"I went to Sweetwater with a ranger from UCIT to make it official."

Chase nodded, knowing protocol was to call in the Unsolved Crimes Investigation Team on this. "So what happened?"

Jesse leaned forward resting his arms on his knees. "Reyes's story is that he knows the man who shot Ranger Wade Landon."

"So who is it?"

"He says he'll only talk if the D.A. will make a deal."

Chase didn't like the sound of this. "Let's see, Reyes is a known drug dealer. He's in for armed robbery, then add on a kidnapping charge, attempted murder and… he's a horse thief."

"It was Jacobs who shot Buck Kendrick," Jesse clarified. "Also Reyes swears he's the one who kept Ryan safe."

Chase hated to think what could have happened to his

son. Ryan was safe now, and he was going to make sure of that. Men like Jacobs and Reyes needed to stay off the streets.

"Reyes says the drug dealer who shot Wade is big time," Jesse explained. "He also hinted that the man likes to collect trophies of his kills." Jesse's gaze never wavered. "Like guns…and a Texas Ranger's badge."

Chase froze. No one had that information but law enforcement. "What's your gut tell you about this guy?"

"Reyes is scum," Jesse said. "But…he's small-time scum. Reyes knows he's not getting out anytime soon. But he wants a deal where he can be moved to a facility closer to his mother so she can visit him…and take off the life sentence. He wants a straight twenty years, with the possibility of parole."

Chase shut his eyes for a moment. "What's the prosecutor say?"

"Nothing, yet. He needs a name and enough proof that he can bring in the killer and get a conviction."

Chase knew he couldn't ignore this. Over the years he'd followed too many leads that never went anywhere. He had to talk to Reyes. "I'll be back in Midland this afternoon. Tell UCIT I'll be ready to go first thing in the morning."

Jesse nodded. "We'll be ready."

Just then there was another knock on the door. "Come in."

A smiling Ryan stepped into the room and went right to Chase. "Mom and Liz want to know if you both want breakfast?"

The men exchanged glances and nodded. "Sounds good."

Ryan looked at Jesse. "Did you know that Chase is my dad?"

"Really?" Jesse exchanged a knowing glance with Chase. "How great is that?"

"And we're building a tree house, too. It's almost finished." He looked at Chase. "Dad, are we still going to work on it after breakfast?"

Jesse motioned for the door. "I'll head on downstairs to wash up."

"Tell Mallory I'll be down in ten minutes." After Jesse left, he looked at Ryan. "Sit down, son. I have a favor to ask you."

"Sure." The boy sat on the mattress next to his dad. "What's the matter?"

"Remember the guys who kidnapped you?"

He nodded. "Are they still in jail?"

"Yes, but the man named Reyes has some information about the guy who shot another Texas Ranger. Remember when I told you my uncle Wade took the place of a father who wasn't around?"

The boy nodded.

"Well, he was also a Texas Ranger. He was shot and killed about ten years ago." Chase felt a strange surge of emotion. He also felt Ryan's hand in his. "When I buried him, I promised that I'd find out who killed him. This man Reyes might know something. He wants to talk to me tomorrow morning."

"So you have to leave today."

"It's my duty, Ryan. I'm a Texas Ranger. If it wasn't important, I wouldn't leave you."

"I know." There were tears in the boy's eyes, and his lower lip trembled. "Are you coming back…to see me?"

Something tightened around Chase's heart. "So many times that you'll probably get tired of me."

Finally Ryan smiled. "I never will. You're my dad. I love you." He hugged him tightly.

"And you're my son. I love you, too."

He looked up. Mallory was standing in the doorway, and a mountain of emotions bombarded him. And they weren't just for Ryan. He wanted to enclose her in the same hold he had on his son, and keep them both close forever. The thought surprised him, but even more, it scared the hell out of him.

The realization suddenly hit him; he wanted it all. His son, Mallory…a complete family. Just how could he convince her to take a chance on him again?

Mallory fought to find her voice. "Ryan, why don't you go downstairs and help Liz so your dad can shower?"

"Sure." He turned back to Chase. "Don't take too long, we're fixing pancakes."

He smiled. "I'll make it fast." He mussed the boy's hair, before he took off, leaving them alone.

Mallory wasn't sure what to say to him this morning. Then Chase took it out of her hands as he walked to her, pulled her into his arms and kissed the daylights out of her.

By the time he released her, she had trouble catching her breath. "Good morning," he whispered.

"Morning," she labored to answer.

"I could have greeted you a little more up close and

personal, but you disappeared from bed before I got the chance."

"I thought it was better if Ryan didn't catch us…his imagination would run wild."

His lazy grin appeared and her heart began to pound hard once again. "I know the feeling. My own imagination is going a little crazy. Damn." He sighed deeply. "Last night was incredible."

Mallory could feel the blush rise to her cheeks as she thought about their wonderful night together. She'd done the unthinkable. She'd fallen hopelessly in love with Chase Landon. Again. Not a smart thing.

"Yes, it was, but…we have to think of Ryan, too." She pulled back. "It might be better—"

He placed a finger against her lips. "Don't create problems, Mallory. We can work this out."

She stiffened, then stepped back. "Working this out means exactly what? That you come on weekends to spend time with your son, and I'm a bonus."

She saw the anger flash in his eyes. "That's what you think of me…and what we shared last night?"

Mallory knew she had come on too strong. She was frightened, too. "I'm sorry. It's just that we've all spent an idyllic two weeks here…no outside problems to interfere with it. Real life isn't like that. It'll be a huge struggle, Chase, just for you to be able to spend time with Ryan. We don't even live in the same town."

He raked his fingers through his hair and walked to the other side of the room. The muscles worked across his broad back and shoulders. Her gaze moved to his pajama bottoms hung low on his slim hips. More memories flooded her and she wanted to run to him. Beg him not to leave. But she'd done just that nearly ten years ago…and he'd left her anyway. Tears pricked her eyes. She couldn't do it again. This time their son would be hurt.

The following morning, Chase and Hank Whiting from UCIT, along with a D.A., were ushered inside the prison visiting room to talk with Reyes. Chase knew that if this panned out, he could finally close the door on this chapter of his life.

His thoughts turned to Mallory. She'd tried to act indifferent when he'd driven away yesterday, but he saw something else in her eyes. Yet, he knew she'd been right. He couldn't give her any promises, not until his past was settled. And she still had ghosts that followed her, too. Her marriage to Alan had made her leery of giving herself to him…or any man.

Today would change that one way or the other. Whether there was evidence or not on who shot his uncle, he had to let it go. Wade wouldn't want it to take over his life. And yet, it had. Even years ago, when he couldn't commit to Mallory. He wanted so badly for today to change that….

For so many years Chase hadn't wanted any connections. To let people in. For a second time Mallory changed that, but was he too late? Too late for a family. All he knew was he wanted his son and Mallory and somehow he was going to find a way to get them all together.

Chase turned as the metal doors opened and a guard entered with Reyes. The prisoner didn't look happy. He nodded to Chase. "I only wanted to talk to the ranger."

"Cut the crap, Reyes, and get down to business,"

Sergeant Whiting said. "Ranger Landon is here to hear your big news."

In the end, Chase sat down at the table with the prisoner while the other men went to stand with the guard. "Okay, Reyes," he began, "Talk to me. Tell me who killed Wade Landon."

He pointed to the D.A.. "Is he willing to make the deal I asked for?"

"He's willing if you come up with a name and some proof."

Reyes leaned forward and lowered his voice. "Give me a piece of paper."

Chase removed a small pad and pen from his shirt pocket and slid it to the man.

Reyes wrote down something. "My cousin has all the information on this man." He pushed the folded paper over.

Chase opened it and saw a name, Sancho Vasquez. Chase tried not to react, but it was difficult not to. This man was a well-known drug dealer along both sides of the border.

"So why are you giving him up now?"

"He betrayed me," he said, his voice low. "I was a loyal *amigo,* then he hooked my brother on the hard stuff. He was supposed to look out for *mi familia* with me in here. I kept my mouth shut too long.

"Talk to my cousin, Cesar Reyes." He wrote down the information. "He'll tell you about the man's trophies. You'll find what you're looking for."

"You better not be jerking my chain, Reyes, or you'll be sorry."

The prisoner raised his cuffed hands in surrender. "You'll be happy. Just get me out of here so I'll be safe."

Chase stood. "As soon as we get our man."

"Then you'll come back and thank me." Reyes grinned. "Is the *niño* okay?"

Chase thought about his son. "Yes, the boy is fine."

It had been a long day by the time Chase turned in to the drive at his town house. After they'd left Reyes, he and Whiting had gone to find the cousin. Late last night, Cesar had met them in a secret location and handed over the information on Vasquez.

The day wasn't over yet. Jesse, Whiting and he were headed down to the border town of Presidio, Texas. Before dawn they were going in to search Vasquez's U.S. headquarters in the Chinati Mountains.

Chase hoped everything they'd been looking for was on this side of the border. It would sure make things easier.

He walked through the door of his home and into the empty silence. It suddenly hit him…along with a hard loneliness in his gut. Hell, he missed his son… and Mallory.

He picked up the phone from the kitchen and punched in the memorized number. By the second ring, it was answered by Mallory saying, "Mooney Ranch."

His throat went dry like a teenager's. "Hi," he managed.

There was a long pause. "Chase," she said in a throaty voice.

"I meant to call sooner, but…things got going and just didn't slow down. I hope I didn't call too late."

"No…it's fine. I just came upstairs to my bedroom."

He bit back a groan, thinking about her lying in bed. He shook away the thought. "How's Ryan?"

"He misses you, of course."

"Believe me, I miss him, too. I would have called sooner, but we were in a meeting most of the afternoon. And tomorrow I leave."

Another long pause. "So you got the information you were hoping for."

"Yes. We're still not sure if it's going to pan out. First, we have to find the man…" He stopped. He couldn't tell her any more, but surprisingly he found he needed to share everything, including his fears, with her.

"Chase…are you okay?" she asked.

He sank down on his oversized sofa, lifting his feet on the coffee table. "I could say I've been better."

"Wade meant a lot to you. I just wish there was something I could do to help."

His chest tightened and he closed his eyes wishing she was with him. "You're doing just fine, Mal. Just fine."

She paused. "Will you promise me something, Chase?"

Anything in the world. "If I can."

"Be careful. I know how much you want this guy, but he's a murderer."

"It's my job to bring him to justice." He didn't want to waste his time talking about Vasquez…he wanted Mallory. "Will you be waiting for me when I get back?"

"Are you coming back here?"

"My vacation time sort of ran out. I thought I'd save those few days." He paused. "Dammit, Mallory, I want to see you. I want to hold you…make love to you."

There was a pause. "I don't think we should talk about this now...."

"It's past time, Mal. We should have been together long ago." He released a breath. "Give us a chance."

"I don't know if I can," she said. He could hear the tears in her voice. "I've found a life I like, Chase. I'm my own person."

"And you can't share it with anyone?"

"I've tried, Chase. And if you care about me, please don't try and push me into anything."

CHAPTER TEN

FOR THE LAST twenty-four hours, Mallory had tried without success not to worry about Chase. She hadn't slept since she'd talked to him on the phone, since she'd lied and told him she didn't want a future with him.

Mallory leaned against her pillow and closed her eyes. She didn't know many of the details about the assignment, but that didn't stop her prayers to keep Chase safe. Although he was well trained at his job, he was still going after a known killer.

Suddenly regrets filled her. What if something happened? What if Chase never came back to her...to Ryan? Tears filled her eyes.

"Mom..."

She sat up and saw her son standing in the doorway to her room. "Ryan...what's wrong, honey?"

"I can't sleep. I'm worried about Dad."

She held out her arms and the boy came to her. He climbed in beside her and let her cradle him close. "It's going to be all right, Ryan. Chase is a ranger, he knows what he's doing."

"I know, but this is a really bad guy." Her son raised his head, and his dark eyes met hers. "He killed someone. Every time I close my eyes I see him shoot at Dad."

She tensed. "I wish I could say he isn't in danger, but we don't know that. Just trust that your dad knows his job, and he wants to come back to you more than anything in this world."

Ryan nodded. "He wants to come back to you, too. Mom, he loves us both."

She swallowed hard. Mallory wasn't so sure. She knew Chase loved his son, but was she just part of the package? He hadn't loved her enough to want her years ago. And she couldn't go through that kind of rejection again….

"Hey, why don't we go and visit Grandpa? You can be closer when your dad gets back home."

His eyes lit up. "Chase will want you there, too."

Mallory didn't want to burst her son's bubble right now. This was all too new. She just wanted them all to get through the next few days. She knew that Chase had waited for years to find his uncle's killer.

Then hopefully, she could get back to her life. But she knew with Chase Landon in it, things would never be the same again.

The next morning at dawn, Chase and Jesse hid behind a large boulder, staking out the Spanish-style house on the ranch compound. Nothing looked suspicious. To the untrained eye, it looked like any of the other ranches in the area.

This was supposed to be Sancho Vasquez's U.S. headquarters. All the big guns were out here today, the

DEA, the U.S. Marshals, along with the Texas Rangers and local law enforcement.

Reyes had better be telling the truth about this place being where Sancho ran his drugs operation across the border through Ojinaga, Mexico. There were several other buildings in the compound, probably housing the drugs. Word on the street was there was marijuana and cocaine stored here camouflaged by herds of cattle.

Chase should be happier about the possible drug bust, but he had one thought on his mind. To get his uncle's killer. Everything else was a bonus.

His phone vibrated on his belt. The text message stated all the men were in place and ready to move in. They had a search warrant in hand, but they knew Vasquez wasn't going to let them just walk in.

"It's time," he told Jesse. "Let's move."

They climbed into their vehicles, along with several rangers and some local law enforcement and drove toward the compound, breaking down the gate as they went. Once stopped, they drew their weapons.

Several of the workers scattered, some pulled guns, but seeing they were outnumbered, surrendered. Chase drove his jeep to the front of the house and jumped out. With Jesse following him, they kicked in the front door.

"Texas Rangers, come out with your hands up," he called. A lone housekeeper walked out, looking terrified.

Jesse spoke to her in Spanish and asked where Sancho was. Sobbing, she pointed down the hall.

Guns poised, Chase and Jesse took off, peering into several rooms along the hallway, before finding a library. Seeing scattered papers, they had a good idea Sancho had been there…and recently.

"Damn, how did he get away?" Jesse asked as he checked the locked windows.

Chase searched the perimeter of the room and found something odd about the built-in bookcase. One set of shelves was slightly ajar. He tugged it open to find a set of stairs and a long narrow tunnel. "He went this way," he said before walking cautiously down the steps, before waiting for backup.

Chase wasn't about to let the man get away. If Vasquez got through this escape route, he could sneak across the border in no time. And they were out of luck if the drug lord landed in Mexico. He could disappear for good.

Feeling his way along the narrow passage with its rough-hewn beams and dirt floor, Chase fought to find his way through the musty-smelling tunnel. There was barely any light, but he didn't care, he wasn't going to stop.

Finally he saw a soft glow of light and heard voices up above outside the end of the tunnel. Chase stopped behind a beam as Sancho rattled off orders in Spanish to two men. It was something about using explosives to close off the exit.

Jesse came up beside Chase and waited until Vasquez and his men climbed out, then the two rangers went after them. Outside in the grove of trees, Jesse called to them to halt, but one man fired at them. Immediately, Jesse's bullet took him down. The other surrendered, but Vasquez took off toward the jeep. Chase went after him and easily tackled the forty-something dealer to the ground, then handcuffed him before he could work up a fight.

Chase pulled the short man to his feet. "You're under arrest, Sancho Vasquez, for possession of illegal drugs and the murder of Ranger Wade Landon."

He frowned. "You are *loco*. I murdered no one," he said with a sneer. "I want to call my lawyer."

As he walked the man back to the house, Chase read him his Miranda Rights. Jesse was with him as they entered the home and were met by the sheriff and Captain Robertson.

"You got him. Good work."

"You can't hold me for long," Vasquez said as he looked around to see his home being torn apart. "You have no right to destroy my *casa*." He cursed in Spanish. "I demand you leave."

Another ranger came through the front door. "Captain, you won't believe what the DEA found in one of the barns. It's a drug warehouse." He looked at Sancho. "Looks like you're going away for a long time."

The man looked panicked. "I demand to speak to my lawyer."

"You'll get your phone call, Vasquez," the captain said, his voice low and controlled, as if trying to hold it together. "But you might want to tell your lawyer that in our search of the house, we've found a lot of evidence…evidence that will keep you off the streets for good."

The man straightened. "You have nothing on me."

"I have to disagree. We found something very interesting. A hidden room." The captain glared at the prisoner. "You're a sick man, Vasquez."

"What hidden room?" Chase asked Robertson.

The captain frowned. "There was another room off the tunnel."

Chase handed Sancho off to another ranger, then returned to Vasquez's office, not knowing if he was more afraid of what he wouldn't find…or what he would find.

He marched into the library to find DEA agents at the base of the steps. He saw the narrow door open. The hidden room that Reyes talked about…the so-called trophy room.

Heart pounding, Chase crossed the room and peered inside. A light illuminated the small area, and the items on display. He moved inside, drawn to the numerous gun racks that were mounted on the wall.

Chase had trouble controlling his breathing as he eyed the weapons. Right away he zeroed in on the familiar sidearm, a 45 caliber Colt automatic. It was exactly like the one his uncle carried in his holster when he was a ranger.

Chase had no way of knowing for sure until he checked the serial number. But in his heart, Chase knew this was Wade Landon's issued sidearm. Then his gaze caught the shine of silver. It was the familiar star badge. He sucked in a breath to see the name Landon engraved across it.

Emotions tore through him as painful as if he'd been shot himself. Sancho Vasquez had killed his uncle over ten years ago, and now he was going to pay for it. Rage nearly took over…along with the need to go and beat a confession out of the man.

Suddenly he felt someone else in the room. He glanced over his shoulder to see his friend, Jesse.

"You okay?" he asked.

Chase shrugged. "It hurts like hell, but it's nearly over." His thoughts turned from his past to his future... his son...and Mallory.

"Are you sure you're going the right way?" Ryan asked his mother from the passenger seat of the SUV. "I can call Dad and ask him the directions again."

"You will not call anyone," she told him. "I can get us there."

Mallory wasn't sure she wanted to find the ranch. She'd waited for three days to hear from Chase, but got nothing. Not a word. Then this morning at her father's house, he'd called her out of the blue. He asked her to bring Ryan and meet him at a place about forty miles away, nearly halfway between Midland and Lubbock.

"Did Dad say why he wanted to see us here?"

"Honey, you know as much as I do," she said, seeing the worry on her son's face.

The boy smiled. "I'm glad he's back and the bad guy is in jail." He turned to her. "I'm going to start a scrapbook. Did you save the newspaper?"

Mallory smiled and nodded. "Yes, I saved it," she told him, recalling how she'd reread the article and studied the grainy picture of Chase as he brought Vasquez in. She knew he'd downplay it, but his son wouldn't be able to contain his pride.

"Look, Mom. There's the sign." Ryan read it off the faded archway. "The Last Dollar Ranch."

Mallory drove further down the road to find a two-story clapboard house with a brick front. The green shutters needed painting. So did the rest of the place. She turned to see other whitewashed structures, plus a faded red barn.

A man came out the door and stood on the porch waving. It was Chase. Her heart kicked into gear as he smiled, and she knew in that instant she would never love anyone like she loved this man.

"Mom, look, it's Dad."

"I see him." She stopped the SUV and Ryan unbuckled and jumped out of the truck. She watched as her son ran off toward the man in the jeans, Western shirt and dark cowboy hat.

Chase made it to the bottom step as his son launched himself into his arms. Good Lord, the boy felt good.

"I've missed you, son," he told him, unable to let go just yet.

"I've missed you, too, Dad." The boy pulled back. "I was worried you might get hurt and not come back."

"Since I found out about you, I'm extra careful." He set his son down. "And we got the bad guy."

"I know, Mom and I have been reading about it in the paper."

"You have?"

"Yeah. Mom even read it twice."

Chase glanced at the woman coming toward them. She was dressed in those slim jeans that made her legs seem a mile long, giving him thoughts he didn't need right now. He redirected his attention to her face, shaded by her dark cowboy hat. She came closer and he saw her smile and that silky dark hair pulled behind her ears.

"Welcome back," she said.

He wanted to pull her in his arms, but resisted. "Thanks. It's good to be back."

Ryan looked up at him. "Dad, why are we here?"

"Well, because I wanted to show you my new home. The Last Dollar Ranch."

"Oh, boy. You live here?"

He nodded, but kept his gaze on Mallory. "I just moved in yesterday. I have a lot of work to do, yet, but the house is solidly built, and there's plenty of room."

"Will I have a room?" Ryan asked.

"Sure. We can go inside and you can pick the one you want."

Ryan cheered, then took off into the house.

Chase slipped his hands into his jeans pockets and turned to Mallory. "I've missed you."

"This last assignment had to be hard on you. How are you doing, Chase?"

He sighed. "A lot better since you showed up."

She glanced away. "Looks like you've been busy. I had no idea you were buying a place."

"I told you I was looking."

"I thought that was a story you just invented for Ryan's sake."

"No, it's something I've always wanted to do. Have my own place." He stepped closer. "I want you to like it, too." He reached for her and was encouraged when she didn't step back. "And I'm hoping you'll want to spend a lot of time here, too." He leaned down and brushed his lips against hers. He heard her soft gasp, and returned for more. This time he captured her mouth in a hungry kiss. He wanted to let her know how much he'd missed her. How much he wanted her. He finally let go.

"How about if we continue this later?" He took her hand. "I want to show you the inside."

Mallory wasn't sure what to do. Chase had her confused, and she desperately needed to keep her head. She'd made mistakes in the past, and wasn't about to jump into anything. Not even for Chase.

They went up the steps together and across the weathered porch floor. He opened the heavy oak door and led her into a huge entry with bare hardwood floors and a staircase to the second floor. There was an antique cut-glass chandelier hanging overhead.

"Oh, Chase, this is lovely." She walked into the living room with a tile and brass fireplace. There was faded wallpaper on the walls, but that could be easily removed and painted a warm color. There was a camel colored leather sofa, a matching chair and a large television.

"You haven't seen the bathrooms and kitchen yet. They need a lot of work. It's one of the reasons I got the place so cheap."

"I think you got a great deal. This house has charm, and great bones."

The sound of footsteps called to them upstairs. They went up to find four bedrooms, a large bath and then down the end of the hall was a master suite.

Mallory stepped into a huge room with a row of windows; underneath was a window seat. A king-sized bed was against one wall with rumpled covers and a long dresser against another. She peered into a side room which at one time must have been a dressing room, now converted into a bath.

"This is wonderful, Chase. This room looks new."

He came up behind her. "It was done about five years ago. Not my style. If I redo it, I'd like one of those spa tubs and a double shower big enough for two people."

Mallory didn't need to think about this man standing naked with water streaming over his body. Suddenly heat surged through her.

"Hey, maybe we should see about Ryan." She turned and walked out, finding her son down the hall in one of the bedrooms.

"Look Mom, I can see the barn and corral from here." He looked past her. "Dad, can I have this as my room?"

"If it's the one you want. Sure."

"Okay, when do I get to stay here?"

She wasn't sure how to answer that. They hadn't sat down and talked about the arrangements. "Your dad and I haven't had a chance to talk about that. And since he doesn't have much furniture."

"Then let's go downstairs and talk about it?" Chase suggested.

Downstairs, they went through the dining room that had a large mahogany table and six chairs with a matching sideboard. "This is yours?"

"My mother's. I had a lot of things in storage. There's some other things, too. I put them in the garage for now."

They ended up in the kitchen where there was a large pine table and four chairs. The maple cabinets were in good shape, the butcher block countertops were scarred from years of use, but Chase had moved in completely, bringing in his coffeemaker, toaster and can opener.

She glanced through the curtainless window, noticing the wind had picked up as dark clouds blocked the afternoon sun. "Looks like a storm is heading our way. Maybe we should leave, Ryan."

"And get caught in the middle of the storm," Chase said. "No way. You and Ryan are staying here."

As she started to argue, lightning flashed in the dark sky. "Why don't I fix us some supper and we can discuss the arrangements for Ryan to come visit," Chase suggested.

"Yeah, Mom. I want to stay here with Dad."

Chase looked at Mallory. "Do you need to be anywhere today?"

She shook her head. "No, but you aren't exactly ready for company."

He grinned at her. "Why do you say that?" He went to the big cupboard and opened it to show her his supply of canned goods, cereal and bread. "I went shopping this morning."

"So you don't have to work?"

He shook his head. "I'm off until Monday."

"Oh, boy," Ryan chimed in. "We can stay overnight."

Mallory tried not to panic. "We can't, honey. We can make it back to Grandpa's house. Besides, your father doesn't have any beds."

"I've got two sleeping bags," Chase argued. "And you can take my bed."

"Cool," Ryan said. "It's almost as good as sleeping in the tree house."

Mallory was ready to argue again, but a loud crash of thunder drowned her out. She glared at a smiling Chase. She was going to get him for this.

She turned her attention to her son. "How about we eat supper, then see if the storm moves on before we decide to stay tonight?"

"But I want to stay, Mom. It will be fun. I never stayed at my dad's house before."

"But I'm not prepared to stay. We don't have any clean clothes."

"I have a washer and dryer and new toothbrushes," Chase volunteered. "You could sleep in one of my T-shirts."

"Yeah, Mom. Please…"

The rain was now sheeting against the windows and they couldn't even see outside. This was definitely unusual weather for this time of year. A freak storm. She looked at father and son, both giving her the same charming grin. She couldn't resist.

"Okay, we'll stay the night, but we need to leave first thing in the morning. I'll call Grandpa to let him know our plans."

The two exchanged a high five, then took off to the garage to find the sleeping bags.

Okay, Chase Landon, you might have won this round, but you're not going to win again. No matter how much she wished she could, she just couldn't trust her feelings for the man.

The storm had cleared out by ten o'clock, but Chase knew Mallory wouldn't make Ryan leave. But lying on the hard floor in his son's bedroom, he wondered if this had been such a good idea.

"Maybe you should ask Mom out on a date," Ryan said into the darkness, then turned on his side and put his head in his hand. "You want to go out with her, don't you?"

The boy never quit. "I think your mother and I are old enough to handle that on our own."

"But you're not doing anything. I know you like her, and she likes you. She got really sad when you were away."

Chase was thrilled with that news. He also knew Mallory's first marriage had been the worst. Hell, the bastard had abused her. He tensed, hating the fact that he hadn't been around to help her. Well, he was now, and he wasn't going anywhere.

"Maybe you should tell her how you feel," the boy said, breaking the silence.

This wasn't something he wanted to discuss with an eight-year-old. "You ever think that your mom isn't ready?"

The moonlight shone through the curtainless window. "Then why does she look at you all the time? She kisses you, too."

And she made sweet-sweet love to him, Chase remembered silently.

"Dad? If I ask you something will you promise not to get mad?"

"You can ask me anything, son."

"Do you love my mom?"

Chase closed his eyes, feeling something grip his heart. He'd never stopped. "Yes, I love your mother. I love her a lot."

"Oh, wow! This is going to be so cool."

Chase raised a hand. "Just hold on, son. How I feel about your mother, and how she feels about me is between us. You have to promise to stay out of it."

"But, I want to help," he said.

He reached out and touched Ryan's shoulder. "Son, when you get older you'll learn that there are some things a man has to do on his own. And this is one of them."

"You mean when I like girls."

"Yes, when you like girls. Now, go to sleep."

"Okay…" The boy flopped back on the pillow and closed his eyes. Chase did the same, praying that he wasn't going to disappoint his son…or himself.

After a few minutes, he heard his son's even breathing and got up. In his boxer shorts, he walked out of the room and down the hall to his bedroom.

He gave a soft knock and waited until the door opened and Mallory appeared. She was wearing his white T-shirt and nothing else. Oh, boy.

"Is something wrong with Ryan?"

"No, I just wanted to see you to say good-night and give you this." He drew her into his arms and captured her mouth in an eager kiss. She moaned, and wrapped her arms around him. By the time he released her they both were breathing hard.

"Chase, we shouldn't…" she protested weakly.

"I know, but I just needed to see you…just to hold you for a little while." In the dim light he searched her face. "We need to talk about our future, Mallory. I just don't want to be in Ryan's life… I want to be a part of yours, too."

She started to speak, but he silenced her with another kiss. "Later, Mallory," he whispered. "Good night." He touched her cheek, then turned and walked away. Hopefully it was the last time he would walk away from her.

CHAPTER ELEVEN

THE SUN WAS BRIGHT the next morning when Mallory got up and found her laundered clothes were neatly folded at the end of the bed. Chase.

She smiled. "I like the service at this hotel," she whispered. There was no denying her feelings for the man hadn't changed over the years, and seeing him with their son just enhanced them.

It could be so perfect….

She quickly stopped the train of her fantasy thoughts. She'd given her heart to Chase Landon once before, and it hadn't been enough…. He had left her anyway.

He was a Texas Ranger, and that would always come first in his life. His dedication had been one of the things she'd loved about him. The other was his love for his son. She just wasn't so sure there was room in his life for her. She'd learned that a long time ago when he'd so easily left her…and never looked back.

Now, she had to think about their son. Ryan deserved a life with his father, and if that became complicated by her and Chase's troubled past, it would ruin it.

Worse, she didn't know if she could survive losing Chase a second time.

Mallory grabbed her clothes and headed to the shower. She needed to get out of here. There were no more foolish dreams of her being included in his life. Sooner or later, Chase would come to realize that to have a good relationship with his son didn't have to include her.

And it broke her heart.

Chase stood at the old stove, spatula in hand. It was after nine and he was more nervous with every tick of the o'clock. He wanted Mallory to come downstairs. Yet, he didn't. He hadn't planned to ask her to share his life quite this soon, but he couldn't wait any longer. He wanted his family with him…always.

"You want another pancake, son?" he asked Ryan, still surprised that he'd discussed his future plans with the eight-year-old earlier that morning.

"Yes, please. They're really good. But Mom still makes the best. Her blueberry pancakes are the best." He took the last bite on his plate as Chase poured four more scoops of batter on the hot griddle.

"I sure hope your mother likes pancakes."

"She does," Mallory said as she walked in.

Chase smiled. All bright and sunny with her dark hair pulled back into a ponytail, she looked cute. Although her face was free of makeup, her cheeks were still rosy.

"But I'll just have coffee this morning. Then I've got to leave for home."

"Aw, Mom, do we have to?" Ryan asked, looking panicked. "Dad wants us to go with him to look at a horse."

Something had changed overnight. Chase could see it in her face. "I thought since you're the expert, you could help me," he coaxed as he took a mug from the cupboard, filled it and handed it to her. "What do you say, Mallory? Will you help me find a good riding mount?"

She took a sip of coffee, but never met his gaze. "I can, but just not today." She took another drink, and looked at Ryan. "I need to get home." She checked her watch. "If you want you can stay here, and I'll come and pick you up tomorrow afternoon."

Chase's stomach dropped. She wasn't staying at all.

Ryan didn't hide his confusion. "Sure... I want to stay...but not without you."

"Sorry, Ryan," Mallory began. "I can't today, but don't let me stop your fun. I'm sure your dad can wash your clothes for one more night." She set down her cup and kissed Ryan. "Now, I'd better go. Call me if you need anything."

Chase watched as she grabbed her purse off the counter and started out the door.

Ryan turned to him. "Do something, Dad. Mom is leaving and you haven't even asked her."

"How can I stop her?"

"Tell her you want her to stay." He climbed off his chair and started pushing him toward the back door.

Chase ended up on the porch as Mallory was getting into the car. "Mallory, wait..." He took off in a jog and managed to reach her before she got in.

She held up a hand. "Look, Chase, we spent the

night. Now, I have to go. You have Ryan here. That's what you want."

He touched her arm. "It's not all I want, Mal. I want you, too. I've always wanted you."

"Please, Chase, don't do this. We tried once, it didn't exactly work out." She drew a breath. "You deserved this time with Ryan…and a lot more." She finally looked at him, tears filling her green eyes. "I'm sorry that I never gave you the chance before—"

"Stop, Mallory. That's in the past. We both made mistakes." He pulled her against him. "So don't run off. We can work this out."

She shook her head, resisting. "And what happens to Ryan if we can't? He'll be the one who gets hurt. I've made some bad choices in the past. I can't do it again. Goodbye, Chase. I'll be back tomorrow to get Ryan."

Before she could get into the truck, Ryan came running out the door, calling her name.

They both waited as Ryan raced to them. "Mom, I changed my mind, I want to go home with you." He looked at his dad when she climbed in the truck and waited. "She needs me to go with her."

Chase was proud his son wanted to be with his mother, he just wished he could find a way to have them both.

"It's okay, son." He hugged him, knowing nothing was going to be okay at all.

"Chase asked you to stay, and you just walked away?" Liz asked.

Mallory sat at the kitchen table. "It's okay, Liz. I know what I'm doing."

"Oh, really. The man—who you love to distraction—asked you to stay and work out a future, and you left? Are you crazy?"

Mallory finally looked at her friend. "No, I'm practical. Chase wants Ryan. He wants me as part of the package. But in the end, we'll get hurt."

"You didn't even stay to find out." Liz pulled out the chair and sat down next to her. "Look, Mallory, not all men are jerks like Alan. You got the possibility of a future with one of the good guys, but you've got to give the man a chance." She sighed. "You love him…just admit it."

She couldn't. She shook her head. "It doesn't matter."

"Yes…it does matter, Mom."

They both turned toward the back door to see Ryan standing there. "Hi, son," she said, wiping her eyes and stood. "I bet you're hungry."

"No, I'm not."

Mallory knew he'd been upset since they left Chase this morning. He hadn't said a word all the way home.

"You need to eat."

"And you need to tell the truth." His fists clenched. "You know Dad loves you, but you wouldn't even listen to him." He ran out of the kitchen upstairs, then they heard the slam of the bedroom door.

Mallory wanted to cry; instead she went to her son. She'd made so many mistakes by not telling Ryan the truth a long time ago. Somehow, she had to convince him that what she was doing now was for the best.

With an encouraging look from Liz, she made her way upstairs, then knocked on his door. Without waiting, she walked in to find her son on the bed.

It broke her heart to see him looking so sad. "Hey, honey. We need to talk about this."

He nodded, then went into her arms. "I'm sorry I yelled at you."

"I know, son." She shut her eyes. "Oh, Ryan, I know these last few weeks have been tough on you."

"For you, too. You've been so sad for a long time." He wiped his eyes. "Then Dad came here."

"It was because of you, Ryan. He loves you. That doesn't mean that your father and I have to be together."

"Why not? You love him and he loves you. Why is that so hard?"

Out of the mouths of babes. "Sometimes life is complicated."

"But Dad is trying to make it better. He bought the ranch so he can be close to us. And he wants to marry you so we can all live together."

Mallory's breath caught. Marry her? Her son climbed off the bed and went to his backpack. He reached inside and took out a black box. He brought it to her. "Dad got you this. He showed it to me this morning before you got up. He said he wanted to ask you to marry him."

Mallory's hands shook as he held the box. "What are you doing with it?"

"He asked me to keep it safe for him. It's really pretty." The child opened the lid to reveal a pear-shaped diamond ring in an antique setting. It was beautiful.

"I bet if you don't like this ring, Dad will buy you another one. He just had this one for a long time. Even before I was born. He said he was going to ask you to marry him when he got out of training."

Mallory swallowed the dryness in her throat. Oh, God. "What did you say?"

"I said that Dad was going to ask you to marry him before I was born. That's why he bought this ring for you. He said it was your favorite kind."

Tears clouded her vision as she reached for the ring. Then it dawned on her she had told him that she liked antique jewelry. "He remembered…"

"Please don't be sad, Mom. And don't be mad at Dad."

Chase had come back for her. He'd wanted to marry her all those years ago. She hugged her son. "I'm not mad, Ryan. But I did manage to make a big mess of things." She pulled back and wiped her eyes. "I think it's time I tell your father how I feel."

The boy finally smiled. "Just ask him, I did. He told me last night that he loved you."

Her chest tightened. "And I love him."

"Then go and tell him."

"I think I will, son. I think it's past time I tell him the truth."

Chase wanted to stay in bed, but the pounding in his head wouldn't let him. He sat up, feeling every beer he'd drunk last night. He needed some aspirin. Pulling back the covers, he went into the bathroom and took a bottle from the medicine cabinet. He turned on the shower and got in to soak away his misery.

But that wasn't going to happen any time soon. When the water turned cold, he shut it off and climbed out to dry off. He pulled on a pair of jeans and a black T-shirt.

He needed coffee, then a busy day of physical work

to help him forget his troubles. He'd already started on the barn yesterday, hoping to have a horse to board. Didn't look like that was going to happen any time soon.

In the kitchen, he managed to make coffee, then by the time he drank his first cup he heard a vehicle pull up.

Great. He didn't want any visitors today. He got up and saw it was a truck attached to a horse trailer. "What the hell..." He pulled opened the back door and walked outside in time to see Mallory climb out of the truck.

Dressed in faded jeans and a pink blouse, her cowboy hat was cocked back off her smiling face. "Good morning," she tossed at him as she continued to the back of the trailer and started to unhitch the gate. There were two horses inside.

He came down the steps. "What are you doing here?"

Her gaze met his. "I promised to show you some horses, but never got around to it."

What was going on? He took her by the arm to stop her. Mistake. He felt her warmth, even through her blouse. He released her.

"You just decided to bring two horses over here this morning.... Out with it, Mallory, because I can't take any more of these games."

She turned serious. "Okay, I used the horses as an excuse to see you."

His chest tightened, as did his gut. "Hell, Mal, you don't need an excuse...ever."

"Are you sure? I didn't think I'd be exactly welcome."

He'd had enough. "Dammit, woman. Just tell me why you've come here." He blew out a breath. "And don't say it was because of the horses."

She swallowed. "I came to ask you something."

"Okay…" He folded his arms across his chest to keep from reaching for her. "What is it?"

She went to the truck and came back with the black velvet box. "When did you buy me this ring?"

"Where did you get that?"

"Ryan said you gave it to him for safekeeping."

He closed his eyes momentarily. It seemed like another lifetime ago, the plans he'd made with his son. "What does it matter now? You told me there's no future for us."

"Please, Chase, tell me."

"It was the first weekend I had free during my ranger training."

"Nine years ago." Her eyes widened. "You were going to ask me to marry you then?"

He nodded. "But I was too late. I came by the ranch and learned you'd gotten married a few weeks before."

"You came back for me," she whispered. "Why didn't you tell me?"

He shrugged. "Would it have made a difference?"

"Yes. You said you had no room in your life for anything except being a ranger. I thought I'd always be second in your life."

"Never." He reached for her and she didn't resist. "I realized I was wrong. I came back because I didn't want to live without you. When I learned about your marrying another guy, I tried to hate you. If you loved me…you would have waited."

"And if you loved me you would have taken me with you," she countered.

"I did love you, Mallory. That's why I walked

away in the first place. You were so young. Then I found I couldn't concentrate, I wanted you with me... always."

Mallory knew she owed it to him to take the next step. "I loved you, too, Chase. Then and now. Forever." Her gaze met his. "Could you forgive me, and love me again?"

He blinked. "Oh, Mallory, you have no idea." His arms wrapped around her, and drew her closer.

"Tell me..." she whispered. "I need the words, Chase."

"I've always loved you, Mallory. For nine years, I've never stopped, and I don't plan to anytime soon." He kissed her, slowly, softly at first, but then it grew intense.

He finally released her. "Let me have the box."

She handed it to him and watched as he took out the ring. Then to her amazement, he went down on one knee. "This isn't exactly how I'd planned this, but I finally got you agreeable, and I'm not letting the chance slip by. I love you, Mallory Kendrick. I have since the day you went speeding by me. I want us to spend the rest of our lives together, raising our son, and having more babies. Will you marry me?"

Mallory was shaking as she managed to nod. "Yes, oh, yes, Chase, I'll marry you."

He slipped on the ring and kissed her hand. Standing, he pulled her into his arms and swung her around.

He finally set her down. "Dammit, woman. You made me work for this one." He grinned. "But you're worth it."

"I'm sorry—"

"No, no more saying that. We both have made mistakes. We'll probably make a lot more over the next fifty or sixty years, but just know I love you, Mal." He kissed her again. "Come on, let's go into the house so I can show you how much."

Mallory resisted being pulled away. "I'm not sure Beau and Scarlet would be too happy about that."

He frowned. "Oh, man. The horses." He immediately went to the trailer and lowered the gate.

Mallory waited for his reaction to the roan stallion and brood mare. "What do you think of my wedding present to you?"

Chase already had the stallion out of the trailer, then the mare. He stood back and looked them over. "They're beauties. Where did you find them?"

"I happen to have connections. And I thought this guy would sire some beautiful foals."

He grinned. "So we're going into the horse breeding business."

Together, they led the horses toward the corral. "That's one of the things I'd like to do." She led Scarlet inside. Unfastening the lead rope, she let the mare run off. Chase did the same with the stallion. "I was hoping we'd start with our own family...and a baby," she said.

Mallory knew she'd taken a lot away from Chase when she'd never told him about Ryan. She'd lost a lot, too. It had cost them both. No more. This was their time.

"Are you sure you want a baby right now?" he asked, looking hopeful. "We haven't even decided where we're going to live."

She smiled. "I thought we'd live right here. You can continue your work as a Ranger. And I can handle my business anywhere I have a computer. Liz is close enough and can visit us, and so is Dad." She stopped.

"Unless you have something else in mind… I just thought since you proposed to me…you wanted—"

He leaned down and kissed her again. "I want you and Ryan any way I can get you. Here, in Levelland…or Timbuktu. And, yes, I want you to be pregnant with my child…again."

She felt a thrill rush through her. "I feel the same way." She leaned into him. "We have a second chance…." She thought about how she'd almost lost him again.

He reached for her. "Come up to the house with me. We'll discuss our future…and how large our family is going to get."

"So are you going to use your power of persuasion on me?"

He grinned at her. "As a Texas Ranger, I am trained as an expert negotiator. And I feel it's my honored duty to work toward the best results for everyone."

She reached up and kissed him. "Just so you know that you're my Texas Ranger."

EPILOGUE

CHASE STOOD by his uncle's grave. *Lieutenant Wade Landon, Texas Ranger. He served Texas and his family with loyalty and honor.*

Months had passed since they'd caught and arrested Sancho Vasquez. Although the man refused to confess to murdering Wade, there were other witnesses eager to make a deal with the D.A. for a lighter prison sentence.

It didn't matter to Chase. He knew the man had killed his uncle, and with the drug and attempted murder charges against him, Vasquez wouldn't see the light of day ever again.

Chase rubbed his fingers over the silver star badge in his hand. The name Wade Landon was engraved across the front. It was over. He could close this part of his life.

"He was proud of you, Chase."

Chase turned and saw Mallory, his bride of three months. They'd had a small wedding at the Lazy K Ranch with friends and family.

"I hope so. I sure was proud of him."

"I'm proud of you, too," she said as she slipped her

arm around his waist. "You're a special man, Chase Landon. Father, husband…lover."

Mallory couldn't be happier if she tried. She touched her slightly rounded stomach. She was ten weeks pregnant.

"How are you feeling?" he asked. "Shouldn't you be sitting down?"

"No. I should be doing everything that I'm doing." She wouldn't take any chances with their baby, but she wasn't going to go to bed for the duration of her pregnancy, either.

"I think you should slow down a little."

"I have a business, Chase. I'm not overdoing it. And when the time comes, I'll stop." She smiled. "Gladly. There is nothing more important than my family." She glanced at her watch. "I think we'd better get home. Ryan is anxiously waiting for us."

They climbed in the truck and drove back to the ranch they'd renamed the Landon Ranch, Mallory K Landon Horse Broker.

They drove through the new gate and saw the freshly painted house. Flowers bordered the rebuilt porch and the trimmed lawn was lush and green.

After painting the inside rooms, Mallory had brought over a lot of furniture, filling the house with warmth and hominess.

Friends and family were coming from all around for today's festivities, Ryan's ninth birthday. The first Chase got to share with his son. And it was going to be the best…for everyone.

Chase reached over and took Mallory's hand. "I love

you." He squeezed it. "Even more for giving me this second baby."

"I love you, too. And I was thinking about names for the baby. If it's a boy how about the name Wade? And if it's a girl we could name her after your mother and mine, Sarah Pilar."

His throat worked to swallow. "I like that idea."

He pulled up at the house and Ryan came running outside. "Mom, Dad, where have you been? Did you get the cake and ice cream?"

"Son, chill," Chase said as he tugged the boy's hat down. "What do you think this is, your birthday?"

They carried the party items into the kitchen where Liz, Rosalie and Buck were busy organizing things.

Chase wanted just a few minutes with Ryan before things got crazy with the party. He took his son and walked him into the living room that had become the family meeting room. It was painted an olive-green. A brown area rug took away the echo and drapes added privacy.

"What do you want, Dad?"

He still got a thrill wherever Ryan called him that. "This is a special day for you…and for me, too."

"I know. It's my first birthday with you."

Chase nodded. "It's also an ending to something in my life. Your mother and I went to collect the things Vasquez had of my uncle's." He took the ranger badge out of his pocket. "This was his star he wore as a ranger." He handed it to his son.

The boy examined it with interest. "Wow."

"I want you to have it, Ryan. I want you to have something of the man I loved and respected."

"Really?" the boy asked.

Chase nodded. "He was part of your family, too. You should be proud of him, he was a great ranger."

Ryan looked at him with those dark eyes. "Thanks, Dad." He hugged him, then walked away, but stopped in the doorway. "You're a great ranger, too. And I'm proud you're my dad."

Chase felt his chest tighten. "Thanks, son. I'm proud of you, too." He released a long breath. "Now, let's get this party started."

Ryan grinned and ran off. Chase was following as he spotted Mallory standing in the dining room.

"A little father-son talk?"

"I just had a gift for him."

"Another one? The new saddle isn't enough?"

"It was Wade's badge."

She smiled. "Later, we might want to confiscate it for a few years to keep it safe."

He nodded and pulled her close to his side. His emotions were so raw. "Oh, God, it's so good to have you with me."

She hugged him back. "I love it, too." She looked at him. "One of the good things about us finding each other—even though it took a bad situation to get us back together—is we know what we've lost. And we appreciate what we've found again."

"All I know is that I never want to lose you or Ryan again," he told her. "You both mean too much to me."

"Don't worry, we're here for keeps."

Chase kissed her. Today, he wasn't thinking about

how many years he'd longed for this. There was no room in their lives for regrets any more, there was only a future of promise and love.

* * * * *

Chapter 1

October
New York City

Nicole Masters was sitting cross-legged on her sofa while a cold autumn rain peppered the windows of her fourth-floor apartment. She was poking at the ice cream in her bowl and trying not to be in a mood.

Six weeks ago, a simple trip to her neighborhood pharmacy had turned into a nightmare. She'd walked into the middle of a robbery. She never even saw the man who shot her in the head and left her for dead. She'd survived, but some of her senses had not. She was dealing with short-term memory loss and a tendency to stagger. Even though she'd been told the problems were most likely temporary, she waged a daily battle with depression.

Her parents had been killed in a car wreck when she was twenty-one. And except for a few friends—and most recently her boyfriend, Dominic Tucci, who lived in the apartment right above hers, she was alone. Her doctor kept reminding her that she should be grateful to be alive, and on one level she knew he was right. But he wasn't living in her shoes.

If she'd been anywhere else but at that pharmacy when the robbery happened, she wouldn't have died twice on the way to the hospital. Instead of being grateful that she'd survived, she couldn't stop thinking of what she'd lost.

But that wasn't the end of her troubles. On top of everything else, something strange was happening inside her head. She'd begun to hear odd things: sounds, not voices—at least, she didn't think it was voices. It was more like the distant noise of rapids—a rush of wind and water inside her head that, when it came, blocked out everything around her. It didn't happen often, but when it did, it was frightening, and it was driving her crazy.

The blank moments, which is what she called them, even had a rhythm. First there came that sound, then a cold sweat, then panic with no reason. Part of her feared it was the beginning of an emotional breakdown. And part of her feared it wasn't—that it was going to turn out to be a permanent souvenir of her resurrection.

Frustrated with herself and the situation as it stood, she upped the sound on the TV remote. But instead of *Wheel of Fortune,* an announcer broke in with a special bulletin.

"This just in. Police are on the scene of a kidnapping that occurred only hours ago at The Dakota. Molly Dane, the six-year-old daughter of one of Hollywood's blockbuster stars, Lyla Dane, was taken by force from the family apartment. At this time they have yet to receive a ransom demand. The housekeeper was seriously injured during the abduction, and is, at the present time, in surgery. Police are hoping to be able to talk to her once she regains consciousness. In the meantime, we are going now to a press conference with Lyla Dane."

Horrified, Nicole stilled as the cameras went live to where the actress was speaking before a bank of microphones. The shock and terror in Lyla Dane's voice were physically painful to watch. But even though Nicole kept upping the volume, the sound continued to fade.

Just when she was beginning to think something was wrong with her set, the broadcast suddenly switched from the Dane press conference to what appeared to be footage of the kidnapping, beginning with footage from inside the apartment.

When the front door suddenly flew back against the wall and four men rushed in, Nicole gasped. Horrified, she quickly realized that this must have been caught on a security camera inside the Dane apartment.

As Nicole continued to watch, a small Asian woman, who she guessed was the maid, rushed forward in an effort to keep them out. When one of the men hit her in the face with his gun, Nicole moaned. The violence was too reminiscent of what she'd lived through. Sick to her stomach, she fisted her hands against her belly, wishing it was over, but unable to tear her gaze away.

When the maid dropped to the carpet, the same man followed with a vicious kick to the little woman's midsection that lifted her off the floor.

"Oh, my God," Nicole said. When blood began to pool beneath the maid's head, she started to cry.

As the tape played on, the four men split up in different directions. The camera caught one running down a long marble hallway, then disappearing into a room. Moments later he reappeared, carrying a little girl, who Nicole assumed was Molly Dane. The child was wearing a pair of red pants and a white turtleneck sweater, and her hair was partially blocking her abductor's face as he carried her down the hall. She was kicking and screaming in his arms, and when he slapped her, it elicited an agonized scream that brought the other three running. Nicole watched in horror as one of them ran up and put his hand over Molly's face. Seconds later, she went limp.

One moment they were in the foyer, then they were gone.

Nicole jumped to her feet, then staggered drunkenly. The bowl of ice cream she'd absentmindedly placed in her lap shattered at her feet, splattering glass and melting ice cream everywhere.

The picture on the screen abruptly switched from the kidnapping to what Nicole assumed was a rerun of Lyla Dane's plea for her daughter's safe return, but she was numb.

Before she could think what to do next, the doorbell rang. Startled by the unexpected sound, she shakily swiped at the tears and took a step forward. She didn't feel the glass shards piercing her feet until she took the second step. At that point, sharp pains shot through her foot. She gasped, then looked down in confusion. Her legs looked as if she'd been running through mud, and she was standing in broken glass and ice cream, while a thin ribbon of blood seeped out from beneath her toes.

"Oh, no," Nicole mumbled, then stifled a second moan of pain.

The doorbell rang again. She shivered, then clutched her head in confusion.

"Just a minute!" she yelled, then tried to sidestep the rest of the debris as she hobbled to the door.

When she looked through the peephole in the door, she didn't know whether to be relieved or regretful.

It was Dominic, and as usual, she was a mess.

Nicole smiled a little self-consciously as she opened the door to let him in. "I just don't know what's happening to me. I think I'm losing my mind."

"Hey, don't talk about my woman like that."

Nicole rode the surge of delight his words brought. "So I'm still your woman?"

Dominic lowered his head.

Their lips met.

The kiss proceeded.

Slowly.

Thoroughly.

* * * * *

*Be sure to look for the **AFTERSHOCK** anthology next month, as well as other exciting paranormal stories from Silhouette Nocturne.*
Available in October wherever books are sold.

nocturne™

NEW YORK TIMES BESTSELLING AUTHOR

SHARON SALA

JANIS REAMES HUDSON
DEBRA COWAN

———

AFTERSHOCK

Three women are brought to the brink of death...
only to discover the aftershock of their trauma has
left them with unexpected and unwelcome gifts of
paranormal powers. Now each woman must learn to
accept her newfound abilities while fighting for life,
love and second chances....

Available October wherever books are sold.

www.eHarlequin.com
www.paranormalromanceblog.wordpress.com

SN61796

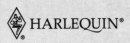

Coming Next Month

**Handsome sheep barons, maverick tycoons and dashing princes—
you can find them all in Harlequin Romance®!**

#4051 BRIDE AT BRIAR'S RIDGE Margaret Way

In the second of the *Barons of the Outback* duet, Daniela Adami comes to Wangaree Valley to escape her life in London. Her heart is guarded, but when handsome sheep baron Linc Mastermann strides into her world, he turns it upside down....

#4052 FOUND: HIS ROYAL BABY Raye Morgan

Crown Prince Dane—the third of the *Royals of Montenevada*—has heard rumors of a secret royal baby. With the kingdom in uproar, his only choice is to confront Alexandra Acredonna—the woman who still haunts his dreams....

#4053 THE MILLIONAIRE'S NANNY ARRANGEMENT Linda Goodnight
Baby on Board

The only thing businessman Ryan Storm can't give his six-year-old daughter is a mom—but he can hire the next best thing.... Pregnant and widowed, Kelsey Mason isn't Ryan's idea of the perfect nanny—but little Mariah bonds with her straight away, and soon he starts to fall under her spell....

#4054 LAST-MINUTE PROPOSAL Jessica Hart

Cake-baker Tilly is taking part in a charity job-swap, but when she's paired with ex-military chief executive Campbell Sanderson, Campbell is all hard angles to Tilly's cozy curves. But something about her always makes him smile. And then they share a showstopping kiss....

#4055 HIRED: THE BOSS'S BRIDE Ally Blake
9 to 5

Mitch Hanover needed a miracle—someone to bring life to his business— and when Veronica Bing roared up in her pink Corvette and told him she was the girl for the job, he couldn't help but agree! But even though attraction zinged between them, Mitch had sworn never to love again....

#4056 THE SINGLE MOM AND THE TYCOON Caroline Anderson

Handsome millionaire David Cauldwell is blown away by sexy single mom Molly Blythe. He can see she and her young son need his love as much as he yearns for theirs—but falling in love means taking risks: David must face the secret that changed his life....

HRCNM0908